"Do you have a name or do you just go by 'bodyguard?'"

The smile toyed with his lips again. "You can call me Pete."

Since talking with him was about as gratifying as talking to a brick wall, Elle changed tactics. Lowering her voice, moving a step closer, doing that thing with her eyelashes again, she added, "Will you help me, Pete?"

"I thought you were afraid of getting shot."

Why was he teasing her? Was he flirting—or suspicious? She hadn't done anything wrong... yet.

Before she could answer, he said, "You'll have to get by me and security guys first. Background search."

"Background search?" She had to relax. A background search would come up empty. She'd appear exactly as she was—ordinary. No one knew her movies.

Her life was on the line and she *would* get answers. And no one—not even a bodyguard in perfectly fitted jeans—was going to stop her.

ALICE SHARPE

AVENGING ANGEL

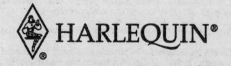

HARLEQUIN®

TORONTO • NEW YORK • LONDON
AMSTERDAM • PARIS • SYDNEY • HAMBURG
STOCKHOLM • ATHENS • TOKYO • MILAN • MADRID
PRAGUE • WARSAW • BUDAPEST • AUCKLAND

This book is dedicated to my mother, Mary R. LeVelle, and my editor, Allison Lyons, both women who know exactly what to say and when to say it.

My special thanks to Alma D. Velazquez for her patient help with translations. Thanks also to my horse experts, my sister, Mary Shumate, and fellow writer, Danita Cahill.

ISBN-13: 978-0-373-69318-4
ISBN-10:   0-373-69318-4

AVENGING ANGEL

Copyright © 2008 by Alice Sharpe

www.eHarlequin.com

Printed in U.S.A.

ABOUT THE AUTHOR

Alice Sharpe met her husband-to-be on a cold, foggy beach in Northern California. One year later they were married. Their union has survived the rearing of two children, a handful of earthquakes registering over 6.5, numerous cats and a few special dogs, the latest of which is a yellow Lab named Annie Rose. Alice and her husband now live in a small rural town in Oregon, where she devotes the majority of her time to pursuing her second love, writing.

Alice loves to hear from readers. You can write her at P.O. Box 755, Brownsville, OR 97327. A SASE for reply is appreciated.

Books by Alice Sharpe

HARLEQUIN INTRIGUE

  746—FOR THE SAKE OF THEIR BABY
  823—UNDERCOVER BABIES
  923—MY SISTER, MYSELF*
  929—DUPLICATE DAUGHTER*
1022—ROYAL HEIR
1051—AVENGING ANGEL

*Dead Ringer

CAST OF CHARACTERS

Elle Medina—She swore to avenge the brutal slaying of her family but didn't count on falling for the murderer's bodyguard. Will she uncover the truth, and if she does, will she have the courage to face *all* its ramifications?

Pete Waters (a.k.a. Peter Walker)—This DEA undercover agent posing as Alazandro's bodyguard is obligated to protect the man Elle is determined to kill. He has a history of falling for self-destructive blondes—is Elle just another woman about to implode?

Víctor Alazandro—He figures his current wealth and power shield him from all of his illegal endeavors. He hasn't counted on Elle Medina's single-minded passion to bring him to justice.

Peg Stiles—Her beloved horse stable is being gobbled up by Alazandro. There's only one way left to stop him....

"The Judge" (Daniel Medina)—Elle's adopted father. What does this man, who was her dead father's friend and police partner for years, know that he isn't telling?

Amber Linn—The young woman whose death months before has everyone at Puerta Del Sol resort wary of bad publicity.

Jorge—He's always lurking, listening. The other stable hands don't like him. Is he just skimming their wages or do his crimes reach further, deeper, darker?

Tom Meachum—A likeable guy but an unlikely stable manager. Elle doesn't trust him. What's he really up to?

Steve—Appalled by the mayhem at the resort, this copilot is willing to fly Elle home at a moment's notice. Should she take him up on his offer?

Alberto Montega—A business associate of Alazandro's. Do his career plans include murder?

Prologue

March, twenty years earlier

Daddy said never open the door to strangers.

Janey shrank back against the wall, holding Teddy tight against her chest, squeezing her eyes shut until the man outside stopped pounding.

She pulled a chair over to the door and climbed on top. Gently pulling one edge of thick drapery away from the inserted glass panel, she peered outside. Gray skies, trees with just a shimmer of green, wet pavement. The man was gone but she could see the edge of a big brown box peeking above the cement step.

Should she open the door and get the box?

What if it was a trick and the man was waiting behind a bush to grab her? She was too smart for that. She'd be six years old pretty soon and she wouldn't fall for a baby trick. She climbed down and pushed the chair back to the corner, still holding on to her bear.

She didn't know how long Daddy had been asleep and she'd been alone. She didn't know where Mommy was or Baby Brother. All she knew was that Daddy was lying down in the basement and she was alone.

And her tummy hurt.

She wandered into the messy kitchen and opened the refrigerator. She'd been eating what she wanted when she wanted it. No one to tell her not to eat cupcakes for dinner. No one to scold her for spilling purple juice on the floor.

She found a bowl of black olives on the bottom shelf and carefully stuck one on the tip of each finger as juice dribbled down her arms. Eating them off one at a time, she chewed thoughtfully while Teddy stared at her from the floor, his lone black button eye shiny and bright.

Her tummy still felt funny.

Hugging Teddy so tight his fur squished between her sticky fingers, she crept to the basement door.

The light was on which was funny because Daddy was so asleep. She wondered if she should turn off the light but she couldn't bring herself to do it. Instead she tiptoed halfway down the stairs and stopped, staring at Daddy's back.

He was lying on the floor, hands tucked under his body, face turned toward the wall. She was glad because she'd looked at his face once and it had scared her.

Why wouldn't he wake up?

"Daddy?" she said, teeth chattering from cold and from something else she couldn't name.

He was so still and quiet….

A big envelope lay on the ground a couple of feet away. It had a funny little smiley face on it.

"Daddy?" she said again.

There was more banging on the front door and this time a voice she recognized.

Janey backed up the stairs, one hand reaching out to touch the wall for balance, her gaze glued to her father's back until he disappeared from view.

Chapter One

August, Present Day

The moment she flew out of the saddle, Elle Medina knew she'd blown it.

Unless Víctor Alazandro hadn't seen the fall. Unfortunately, a running horse stopping short of a fence while the rider kept going had a tendency to draw attention.

She hit the water hazard—filled earlier in the day in preparation for this jumping class—with a splash, landing face down in the murk, wishing she could sink into the ooze and disappear below the Nevada soil, right into the center of the earth.

Instead, she raised her head in time to see the dappled gelding trot off toward the corral fence while her student ran toward her screaming, both hands fluttering at her sides like little propellers.

Tabitha fell to her expensively clad knees, avoiding the splattered muck. "Elle? Are you okay? I can't believe *you* fell off Silver Bells. I've never even done that!" The girl shaded her eyes with one hand as she looked around the corral. "Is he okay?"

Elle, on hands and knees, twisted her torso and

plopped back down on her read end. Shoving fine strands of dripping blonde hair away from her face before resting her forearms on bended knees, she said, "I'm fine, Tabitha, stop fussing. Silver Bells—"

"He just stopped," the girl said. "He just ran up to the fence and stopped. And you…didn't."

"I'm fine," Elle repeated. She didn't add what she suspected was the truth. Silver Bells had probably stopped short of the jump because Tabitha had veered him away at the last minute a half dozen times before Elle took over to demonstrate how it was done. Apparently, the horse had had enough. She added, "Why don't you go tend to Silver Bells."

"Poor baby," Tabitha gushed, springing to her feet.

The *poor baby* in question, reins trailing in the dirt, took one look at Tabitha's frantic approach and trotted toward Mike, the stable hand, who had come to see what the commotion was about.

Elle took stock of her own situation. She might be covered in muddy water, but at least nothing felt broken.

Well, nothing except her pride. Falling off a horse like a blasted rookie. Oh well, get over it. She hadn't been waiting around Tahoe Stables for her big chance just to give up because of a little mishap.

She knew Víctor Alazandro was on the property. She'd seen him and an assistant arrive, but she'd lost track of his exact whereabouts during the lesson. Sometimes Peg took people inside for a quick drink before giving them a tour of the stables. With any luck, Elle could sneak off and change clothes before the promised introduction to Alazandro.

That slim hope died away as she struggled to her feet. Peg, Alazandro and the man who had accompanied Alazandro stood with arms hooked over the corral railing, staring right at her.

Two options. Walk toward them, run away.

Only one option with any chance for salvaging this disaster. Waving a hand at Mike who appeared to have things under control, Elle started walking toward the three onlookers. She straightened her shoulders, held her head high. At five foot five, she wasn't a particularly tall woman and her outdoor life kept her on the slim side, but she walked as though she owned the ground, ignoring her squelching boots, chafing jeans and the mud-splattered T-shirt plastered against her breasts.

Peg Stiles, owner of the stables and Elle's boss, regarded Elle's approach with a rare grin.

Alazandro's hooded dark eyes, however, revealed nothing. A black Stetson crowned a larger than average head and a body still trim and fit. Alazandro was in his forties, newly divorced, reportedly urbane and calculating. He wore a white silk Western-style shirt piped in black. His black boots, buffed to a high polish, sported two-inch stacked heels.

The second man stood a head taller than Alazandro with a loose-jointed, lanky look. Mid-thirties, blond hair cut military short, angular face, shoulders out to there and back. His clothes weren't as pristine as Alazandro's or as rumpled as Peg's. Jeans and a white cotton shirt rolled up at the sleeves, buckskin vest, dusty boots. A silver buckle caught and reflected the same sunlight that had bronzed his skin. He held a disreputable hat in one hand. And his gaze, steady and very direct, made Elle flinch.

She tore herself from this man's scrutiny and turned all her attention to Alazandro just in time to hear him mutter a few words to Peg.

"This is the 'expert' horsewoman you told me about?" he said in a deep, rich voice that held no trace of an accent. No reason it should. His mother had been born in Guadalajara, his father in Rome with both of them emigrating to the U.S. before marrying and starting their large family.

Elle had done her homework.

It was obvious Alazandro didn't care if Elle heard him or not. Directing his next comment to the tall man, he switched to Spanish, and added, *"Ni siquiera puede ella mantenerse arriba de un caballo."* She can't even stay on a horse.

Still on her side of the rail fence, Elle ground to a halt in front of Alazandro. Using the Spanish she'd learned from the ranch hands back home in Arizona, she tossed her muddy head and said, *"Señor Alazandro, para enseñar a los cobardes, a veces uno tiene que ensuciarse la cara."* To teach cowards, sometimes one has to be willing to get one's face muddy.

Peg, whose language skills began and ended with English, looked confused. The tall blond man's upper lip curled. Alazandro's reaction, the one response she cared about, came slowly. His gaze moseyed from her face southward, pausing on her breasts, moving lazily down to her hips.

This kind of sexually provocative perusal would have annoyed the hell out of her had it come from any other man she'd yet to really meet. Coming from Alazandro, however, it renewed a spark of hope. She didn't care if he hired her to muck out stalls or sleep in his bed. As long as he hired her.

She returned his frank appraisal with one of her own, brazenly studying his mouth before meeting his gaze.

Alazandro, again in Spanish, said, *"Me sorprende usted, Señorita."*

He thought her a surprise? He didn't know the half of it. Carefully forming her next words, she said, *"Ikkyou, Misuta Alazandro? Matawa shinki?"*

His eyes grew wide. "You speak Japanese?"

"Hai," she said, yes. No need to mention how little. She wasn't even sure the sentence made sense.

"Fascinating. And what exactly did you say?"

"I asked if you thought I was a surprise or a novelty," she told him.

"Definitely a surprise," Alazandro said. He'd broken his nose sometime in the past and it had mended slightly crooked. It was the only jarring note on his otherwise handsome face. "Perhaps there is more to you than meets the eye," he said. "And what meets the eye is very…interesting. Peg is quite impressed with you."

"Peg is an exceptionally astute woman."

"Yes," Alazandro said. "I know." His plump lips settled into a smug smile as he added, "She had the good sense to let me bail her out of bankruptcy, didn't she? I'll build a resort on the lakefront half of this property that will be the talk of Lake Tahoe if not the western United States."

"How exciting," Elle gushed.

Maybe she was a better actress than she knew, for Alazandro seemed pleased by her phony enthusiasm. She knew how Alazandro operated. Peg Stiles would be lucky to have a horse left when this guy was through with her. There'd be a fancy resort, all right, it was what Alazandro was famous for. Posh amenities, beautiful waterfront settings, the best horses money could buy.

She couldn't let that be her problem.

"Despite what you saw a few minutes ago, I really

am quite adept with horses as well as with…people," she said.

Peg's harrumph reminded Elle that in the preceding few days, Peg had made it clear she resented Alazandro touring what she still considered *her* property. Peg also hadn't wanted to introduce Elle to Alazandro. It had taken two weeks of pleading to convince her.

Alazandro's voice lowered as he leaned a little closer. "Peg is enthusiastic about your…prospects."

Elle came close to batting her eyelashes as she murmured, "I hope she's not the only one."

Pushing a beat-up hat away from her high forehead, Peg looked from Elle to Alazandro and back again. Years of a two-pack-a-day habit had etched sprays of fine lines into her lean face. She barked, "Hey now, what's going on? I just said Elle here was damn good with horses and is hankering for a change of scenery. Been talking about that new place of yours down in Mexico. This conversation sounds more like cocktail-party crap than serious—"

"Calm down," Alazandro said. Turning his attention back to Elle, he added, "Tell me, Ms.—"

"Medina," Elle said, beginning to extend a hand then remembering her current grimy condition. Hooking both hands in her back pockets, she added, "Elle Medina."

"Tell me, Ms. Medina," he purred. "Do you have any more surprises up your sleeve?"

This elicited a smile from Elle who said breathlessly, "Of course I do. Don't you?"

His laugh was polite. "Oh, yes. Definitely."

Her mind raced as she tried to think of something else provocative to say. She couldn't come up with a darn thing.

Alazandro took Peg's arm. "Okay, *compañera*, show me your stables. Convince me I don't need to tear them down and rebuild them."

"They're fine as they are," Peg snarled, her gaze drifting toward the lake and the trails that crisscrossed her land. Trails her late husband had cleared with his own hands two decades before. The cost of saving at least part of her stable would be losing the much beloved trails. Peg's face reflected the bitterness of this compromise.

For a moment, Elle's sympathy for Peg's plight all but chased her own agenda out of her mind. For a moment, she wished she could stay here and help Peg find a way to make her part of this bargain more palatable. But if this ploy to capture Alazandro's attention failed, she'd have to devise another. And if that failed, another. One way or the other, she was going to get at the truth. She'd promised her grandfather. She'd promised herself.

"You have another appointment in two hours," the blond man said, addressing Alazandro. It was the first time he'd spoken and Elle glanced at him.

He'd put his hat back on his head. She caught him staring at Peg, eyes narrowed.

Alazandro said, "Then let's get to it."

Elle, momentarily caught up in the undercurrents whizzing by, finally realized Alazandro had begun walking away.

"Mr. Alazandro," she called. "Wait—"

Without looking back, Alazandro nodded very slightly toward the blond man who turned to Elle.

She put a foot on the bottom rung of the fence to heave herself over. "But—"

A very tanned hand clamped down on the rail next to hers. She lowered her foot as she looked up. Eyes the color and depth of Lake Tahoe regarded her from beneath the brim of the battered Stetson.

"I need to talk to Mr. Alazandro," she mumbled.

"Isn't that what you were just doing?"

His examination made her uncomfortable and she averted her eyes. "Damn. I blew it."

"Blew what?"

"My chance to get a job at Alazandro's new resort. Of all the days to fall off a horse."

The stranger seemed to reach a conclusion of sorts, as though finding a missing piece of a troubling puzzle. "So you really are after a job," he said. "Hence the language demonstration. But why Japanese?"

"I've heard he gets a lot of Japanese tourists at his resorts. I thought someone working in the stable who could communicate with the visitors as well as with the local staff might come in—handy."

"Puerta Del Sol doesn't open for several weeks," the stranger said. "After hurricane season."

Door of the Sun. Such a peaceful name for a resort beside the sea. So misleading. Never mind, all Elle knew for sure was what she'd overheard Peg telling her lawyer. Alazandro was headed down to Mexico after his visit to Peg's stables. One way or another, Elle was going, too.

"I know when it opens," she said. "But there must be a lot of work going on beforehand, right? Trails to map and clear? Horses to feed and exercise?"

His eyebrows furrowed. "And you want to do that kind of grunt work?"

"I'll do whatever it takes," she said.

Staring right into her eyes, he said, "Why? What's so important to you about getting hired for the Puerta Del Sol resort?"

She hadn't expected this question, especially coming from him. After a ten second delay, she said, "I like learning about…things."

"So your interest lies in resort management?"

"Maybe." Hoping to win back control of the conversation, she added, "I don't know how to apply a mud pack, my tennis game sucks and I know zip about deep-sea fishing. My options are limited. But I do know horses."

"I see," he said, his upper lip lifting a hair as he looked at her. She knew what he saw. The mud, the dripping hair. The anxiety. She started to explain about Tabitha and the jump and the disgruntled horse and thought better of it. She'd already said enough.

Chancing another glance at his face, she said, "Who are you, anyway?"

"Who do you think I am?"

"I don't know. A secretary, maybe?"

"Do I look like a secretary?"

"Do you ever just answer a question?" she snapped.

"Sometimes. Do you?"

She glared at him until she remembered that he had accompanied Alazandro and so might exert a certain amount of influence. It wouldn't pay to push him too far.

As she tried to think of a graceful way to back down, he said, "I'm Alazandro's bodyguard."

"Why does Alazandro need a bodyguard?"

"He's a wealthy man."

"In other words, someone is trying to, what? Kidnap him? Rob him?"

"Not exactly."

"Then what?"

The bodyguard studied her face. Damn, that way he

had of looking past the surface was getting on her nerves. He finally said, "He recently received a death threat."

The blood drained from her face. If Alazandro died before she had a chance to discover the truth—

"What's the matter?" he said, reaching out a hand to steady her.

"This death threat. Did it come from someone here in the States?" Why did she suddenly feel there was a gun pointed at her back? She had to will herself not to swivel around and look.

"Does it matter?"

Biting her lip she said, "Maybe someone is after him right now. Maybe someone has a gun trained on you. I'm standing awfully close."

"And you don't want to get shot by mistake?"

"No."

"Can't say as I blame you."

"So, who made this death threat?"

His eyes narrowed fractionally as he rested both hands on the top rail. "There you go with the questions again."

She blinked a couple of times. "I'm just curious. I've never met a real bodyguard before."

He didn't reply and she felt herself squirming under his watchful gaze. "I thought bodyguards wore dark suits and sunglasses and those little ear pieces," she mumbled.

"You're thinking of the guys on television."

"So you've been hired to protect him."

"That's what a bodyguard does."

"With your life?"

He half smiled. "He's not the president of the United States."

"So, not with your life."

He stared at her without responding.

"So what does being Víctor Alazandro's bodyguard entail? Are you with him night and day? Do you taste his food before he does?"

The corners of his mouth twitched. "Something like that."

"Do you have a name or do you just go by the designation *bodyguard*?"

"And yet more questions."

"Is your name a secret?"

The smiled toyed with his lips again. "You can call me Pete."

As talking with him was about as gratifying as talking to a brick wall, she changed tactics. Lowering her voice, moving a step closer to the rail, fluttering her eyelashes, she added, "I need to talk to Alazandro about a job before he leaves here today, Pete. Will you help me?"

"You don't need my help," he said, backing away from her as though just remembering his duties lay elsewhere.

"Yes, I do," she said, climbing up on the fence. "Please, wait—"

"You don't need me to put in a good word for you," he insisted. His gaze traveled down her chest and back again, a smile lingering on his lips. "You had him with the wet T-shirt," he said. "You didn't need the Japanese, though it was a nice touch."

The fact that she'd apparently broken into Alazandro's inner sanctum coupled with Pete's quick but thorough perusal shattered what little there was left of Elle's aplomb. She almost fell off the top of the fence. Finally finding a perch, she blurted out, "Then I have a job?"

"You still want a job?"

"Of course."

"I thought you were afraid of getting shot."

"No," she said. "Yes. I mean, I don't want to get shot, of course, but I do want to travel to Mexico, I do want to see Puerta Del Sol."

"And there's no other way for you to afford such an experience, right?"

Why was he toying with her? Was he flirting? Was he suspicious? Of what? She hadn't done anything wrong except fall in a glorified puddle and act like a floozy. Yet. She mumbled, "As a guest? At a thousand dollars a day? I don't think so."

"You have to get by me first," Pete said.

"By you? I don't understand—"

"Me and the security boys. Background search," he added and, tipping his hat, turned on his heels and strode off toward the stable his employer had disappeared into minutes before.

Background search? Her mind raced as she studied Pete's retreat, the way he looked in jeans and his long-legged stride both as troubling as the slight bulge above his waistband that pooched out the back of his vest. She knew what a bodyguard would carry in such a spot.

Damn. He was armed.

Of course he's armed, you dummy, he's a blasted bodyguard! And before that he was probably in the military or a cop or something.

The trick would be to stay off his radar, that's all. If she played her cards right, she'd never fall under his watchful gaze again.

Until it was too late.

No, don't think too far ahead....

She shoved trembling hands in her pockets. Now that Pete was gone, the enormity of her success hit full force.

She slid to the ground and leaned against the fence, fighting to get her heartbeat back to normal.

She told herself the background search would come up empty. She'd appear to be exactly what she was, a twenty-five-year old college graduate who had loved horses her whole life, a woman taking a break before finishing graduate school.

Just an ordinary woman. No one knew her motives.

Except her grandfather, and they'd made a pact.

More worrisome than the background search was news of a death threat. A frown tugged at the corners of her mouth as she pushed herself away from the fence.

Someone else was out to get Alazandro.

She'd have to work fast.

Chapter Two

Pete Walker, a.k.a. Pete Waters, turned at the stable entrance and looked back over his shoulder in time to catch Elle Medina push herself away from the fence and take off toward the barn on the far side of the corral.

Funny that she'd stood there a while.

He entered the stable, pausing for a moment to let his eyes adjust to the dim light. Alazandro and Peg Stiles had made it halfway down the walkway. All along the corridor, horses looked out of their stalls as though curious about the visitors. A palomino close to him whinnied as it tossed its head. The horse reminded him of Elle Medina. Same fair coloring, same liquid brown eyes.

This job was complicated enough without some sexy little bombshell getting in the way.

Did she have any idea what Alazandro really wanted with her? The mud hadn't distracted a bit from her looks. Hard to tell about her hair, but she sported a curvy figure that looked great in skintight wet clothes and a face pretty enough to pay her bills. And she was young. Alazandro appreciated nubile young women with flawless skin and tight little bodies, women burning with the desire to please.

Judging from her behavior, Elle Medina knew what Alazandro had in mind and welcomed it. Some women were like that, turned on by power and money and he guessed she was one of them.

What did it matter to him? If she passed a routine background check, what she and Alazandro proceeded to do or not do was none of his business.

He had bigger fish to fry.

And yet, there was something about her. She was different from Alazandro's other conquests, her sexuality provocative but clumsy as though there were two separate women inhabiting the same body. One, a flirt, a seductress. The other, nervous, fidgety, full of questions, anxiety behind her eyes.

His brow furrowed as a thought raced through his mind, retraced its steps, and sat down to stay. *Maybe he could capitalize on this woman's willingness to be used by a man to further his own goals.*

He paused for a second, absently running a hand down the palomino's nose.

He wouldn't put Elle in danger, of course. Well, not overtly. And if danger arose, he'd be close by to protect her. He wouldn't let her be hurt which was a lot more than Alazandro could or would say.

Okay, okay, it wasn't very nice of him to think of using her this way. But the world Elle had just thrust herself into didn't allow for such old-fashioned concepts as fair play and decency. She thought she was flirting with a wealthy entrepreneur, a playboy, a man who could shower her with all the best money could buy. She didn't know about his drug connections or about the evil rumors that had followed this man for years.

No matter. The hungry way Alazandro's dark eyes had devoured Elle Medina was too big a gift to ignore. And the wave of disgust that interest engendered in Pete just didn't matter.

Pete took a cell phone from his pocket and turning his back to the others, punched in a few numbers. It rang only once before it was answered. Using the palomino's golden head for cover, he lowered his voice. "It's me. I have someone I need checked out right away. Name, Elle Medina. Age, early twenties. Currently working at Tahoe Stables on Lake Tahoe. I'll call back in an hour."

Pocketing the phone, he caught up with Alazandro and Stiles. The former, expounding his plans, talked about tearing down the old stable and replacing it with "something decent." Something with a heated, bigger indoor arena in which to exercise the horses and amuse the patrons as winters were cold and snowy at this elevation. Perhaps an attached arcade with viewing rooms looking down over the arena. Better footing in the arena. Quality work. Something family friendly.

Peg Stiles looked mad enough to string up a rope and hang Alazandro from an overhead rafter.

Pete took his place, hanging back, appearing watchful while his mind raced along twisted paths.

If Elle Medina checked out okay, she might prove to be the key he'd been looking for. Alazandro was going to Puerta Del Sol for a reason that surpassed his stated goal of looking around to see how things were progressing. He had minions to do that for him, though it was true he'd just fired his latest in a string of resort managers. Rumors were flying that a meeting of some kind was in the offing.

But Pete couldn't get close enough to pin down any dates or names.

He needed a way to get closer to the man. To find out—

"Did you call my security people?" Alazandro demanded. "Did you start a background search on the girl?"

Pete blinked away his thoughts and answered, "Not yet. Sir."

A flash of irritation ignited the man's eyes for just a moment. Alazandro was used to getting what he wanted when he wanted it. He said, "Make sure she has a passport. I want her to fly south with us tomorrow on my private jet. That Meacham fellow is proving to be a pain in the neck. I should never have hired him."

"I'll get right on it, sir." Pete all but fawned. He hated this job.

Peg Stiles said, "Isn't this all happening kind of fast? Your fancy resort doesn't open for a while yet. What's the rush? Elle will be hard for me to replace. The season is almost over—"

"Elle Medina is just what I need down there. Bright, pretty, trilingual. She's perfect."

Stiles, going on sixty, had the wiry look of a woman who rarely sat unless it was on the back of a horse. Pete knew she was recently widowed. From the look of her, he'd guess she'd put as much heart and soul and elbow grease into this place as her late husband had. He'd glanced around the inside of her house when they first arrived and found old furniture, worn-out carpets and antiquated appliances. The barn they stood in was swanky by her standards.

The woman was invested in this property. And she was losing it, and she knew it.

Measuring her words, Peg said, "I wouldn't want to hear you took advantage of that girl. Her father is some big judge down in Arizona. If he found out she was being used—"

Alazandro laughed. "You're the one who pointed her out to me. You're the one who extolled her virtues."

Peg bit the inside of her cheek before grudgingly admitting, "Yeah. Well, she kept bugging me."

"Come, *compañera*," Alazandro said in what Pete privately termed his schmoozing voice. "She'll make three times the money. She strikes me as a woman who knows what she wants. Her father is no concern of mine."

With that, Alazandro strode down the walkway toward the rectangle of daylight at the other end. Peg Stiles stared after him for several seconds before visibly forcing herself to follow.

Punching the number for Alazandro's security firm into his cell phone, Pete sauntered along a moment later. He didn't want to keep the boss waiting.

BEFORE TAKING A SHOWER and changing her clothes, Elle made her way to the smaller stable to check on Silver Bells. The gray gelding, coat brushed to a silver shine, had been restabled and was drinking out of his trough. She let herself into the stall and, perching on her heels, ran a hand down each beautiful leg, just to make sure he hadn't hurt himself.

Of course, he wasn't the one who had actually hit the ground. He regarded her with big brown eyes as water dripped from his chin whiskers.

"What are you looking at?" she said as he nibbled at

her hair. She reached up and stroked his soft muzzle. He really was a big sweetie.

"Hey, what happened out there?"

Elle looked up to find Mike standing in the doorway, his thick red hair going every which way as usual. Two sets of dimples and a ready smile didn't hurt his popularity with the female clients. In fact, Elle suspected Tabitha had a big crush on Mike who, at nineteen, seemed embarrassed by her adulation.

"Silver Bells took out his annoyance with Tabitha on me," she said, wondering for a moment if her own distracted state hadn't contributed to the horse's refusal to jump. "Where is Tabitha, anyway?"

Mike rolled his eyes. "Her father finally showed up and took her home. She asked me to tell you she'd see you next week. Oh, and you got a phone call earlier."

Elle's imagination immediately provided a worst-case scenario. Rising, she whispered, "Was it Scott?"

"Who's Scott?"

"My grandfather's nurse.

"Oh. Well, no, it was your dad who called."

"Did he mention Grandpa?"

"No. He wants you to meet him down at the Lakeside Inn at eight o'clock tonight."

"He's here? In town?"

"I guess."

Elle felt like stamping a foot. "What lousy timing."

"He sounded like a nice guy," Mike said.

Elle shrugged. "The judge and I don't see eye to eye about certain…things. That's all."

"Yeah. My dad wants me to be a lawyer. He can't understand why I want to waste my time with horses."

"I know. Mine was livid when I delayed grad school to take care of my grandfather."

"Your grandfather is back in Arizona, right? If you're taking care of him, what are you doing here?"

"We hired a live-in nurse, a big strapping guy."

"Scott."

"Right. They didn't need me so I'm taking a break." Elle didn't add that this go-getter had happened into her grandfather's life at a precarious point in more ways than one. As her grandfather's health had declined, his past regrets had escalated. He'd started rethinking his acceptance of his daughter and her family's unsolved murders, gotten Elle involved, and when Scott mentioned he had a brother working as a detective in the Seattle police department, Grandpa had roped him in.

She realized Mike was talking and tried to get her mind back on track. When he paused, she took the opportunity to get away. "I'm going to hit the shower. I have one more appointment at six o'clock. Let's give Silver Bells the rest of the day off. Would you mind saddling Corky for the student and Majordomo for me?"

"Sure thing, they'll be ready when you are."

Elle emerged back into the sunshine. Her muddy clothes had begun to dry, which made walking a stiff-legged affair. As she started up the slope to her cabin, she thought about how great a shower would feel.

And then—well, she had to figure out a way to get rid of her adopted father, a man she'd nicknamed the judge when he took a seat on the Butter Gulch County bench a few years earlier. What did he want? Hadn't they hurt each other enough the last time they quarreled?

She heard a door bang shut and turned to find Peg striding up the gentle rise toward her, cigarette smoke circling her head. She wore an expression Elle had never seen before.

"Need to talk to you," Peg said, taking the cigarette from her mouth, flicking it to the ground and thoroughly grinding it out with her boot.

"What's wrong?"

"You," Peg said, expelling the last of the smoke. "You're what's wrong."

"I don't understand—"

"What in tarnation do you think you're doing?"

Somewhat startled, Elle blinked a couple of times and said, "You mean asking Alazandro for a job?"

"Yeah."

"Well, I guess I'm moving on. I told you I wouldn't stay for long when I took this job."

"Moving on, is that what you call it?"

"Don't worry, I'll stay here long enough to help you hire someone else."

"You might not be here long enough to find me a replacement," Peg said. Looking at the ground, she shook her head in an almost defeated way.

"Mike is really good with people as well as horses," Elle said gently. "Let him take over."

Peg's gaze flew back to her face. "You think it's the damn job I'm worried about? The job is just part of it. The way you acted with that man—the way you came on to him. I never in my life thought you were that kind of girl."

Elle murmured, "It's not how it looks, Peg."

"I'll tell you how it looks," Peg said. "It looks like you're either a scheming gold digger or a stupid little tart. Either which way, that man will eat you for breakfast and spit you out. I bet he's older than your own father!"

Elle's hands bunched at her sides. She had to fight to control her temper as she said, "I know what I'm doing."

"Do you? All that bastard wants is to get into your pants, you do know that, don't you? And you all but gave him an engraved invitation."

"You are not my mother," Elle said, voice trembling.

"No, and right now, I'm glad I'm not."

Elle turned on her heels and stalked up the hillside, leaving Peg in her wake.

She'd been so caught up in herself she hadn't stopped to fully consider what her behavior would look like to those on the sidelines. She glanced over her shoulder in time to see the screen door slam behind Peg.

Drat. Was everyone she knew going to end up angry with her?

It's not too late, her subconscious whispered. *You can walk away right now.*

But she couldn't.

She couldn't live anymore with her nightmares, couldn't bear the thought that Alazandro remained free to roam the earth while her family lay long dead in their graves. Besides, she'd promised her grandfather she'd find the truth and, if need be, exact revenge.

The sun seemed to dart behind the high clouds as Alazandro's image loomed in her mind. The dark, empty eyes. The crooked nose. The cruel lips. Arrogance dripping out of every pore as he toyed with Peg, toyed with *her.*

And then there was Alazandro's bodyguard, Pete, a man who looked as dangerous as Alazandro, perhaps more so for it didn't appear he had Alazandro's ego to fog his vision. Pete might not admit he'd die for Alazandro but there wasn't a doubt in Elle's mind he would kill for him.

Desperate to get into the hot shower and stop her bone-rattling shakes, she unlocked the door and stripped on the way to the bathroom. She stood under the hot water for a long time, eyes closed, hands propped on the tile walls, head hung, caught in the aftershock of her audaciousness.

ELLE MEDINA didn't lock her door.

Stupid.

Pete frowned for a second because if there was one thing Elle didn't strike him as it was stupid. Reckless, absolutely, but not stupid.

He could hear the shower running—made a nice way to keep track of Elle while he had a quick look around. All he had to do was keep his mind on his job and off visions of her all wet and soapy.

The few pieces of furniture in the place looked like castoffs from Peg Stiles' house down the slope. A line of clothes and boots strung across the floor from the doorway to the closed bathroom door sounded the only note of discord in the otherwise orderly space.

He tossed her place quickly and thoroughly, searching drawers, closets, behind mirrors, under the bed. As the cabin was little more than a studio apartment, it didn't take long.

The first conclusion he reached was that the woman had fewer clothes and shoes than any other woman he'd ever known. Heavy on jeans and T-shirts, boots and knee-high socks. Even her nightgown was white cotton. Nothing sexy about it except if you stopped to think what it might look like flowing around Elle's curves.

Enough of that. But still, he'd been married once in his

dim youth to a strawberry blonde whose closet rod sagged in the middle.

The last woman he'd cared about was another type altogether. She'd maintained a working wardrobe toward the end. Big on thigh-high boots and halter tops and tiny shorts that showed more than she ever understood. Showed malnutrition. Showed neglect. Showed the absence of rounded flesh and ripe possibility.

Drugs will do that to a woman. Whisper in her ear, tell her she's gorgeous while robbing her blind.

He hung Elle's gown back on the hook beside the one holding up a blue terry cloth robe. He found her purse on a shelf in the closet. Identity matched, checkbook in her name, nice photo on her driver's license, made her look sixteen years old. According to the data, she was actually twenty-five and wore contact lenses. He hadn't noticed them when he peered into her big brown eyes.

Still holding her purse, he gazed through the window and got his first troubling sensation about Elle. Okay, that wasn't true, she'd been troubling him ever since he laid eyes on her.

His contact had verified her father was a judge in some hole-in-the-wall town in Arizona. Raised on a small ranch. Mother dead. Only other living relatives a smattering of cousins, two aging aunts in New Jersey and a grandfather with terminal cancer. She'd graduated with a degree in public relations, applied for and been accepted to graduate school, dropped out to live with her ailing grandfather. Then she'd suddenly left his bedside to come to Nevada and take a low-paying job giving riding lessons to little girls.

Odd. But not criminal.

He suddenly realized the shower had stopped.

Elle's voice came next, low and serious. "Drop my purse, put your hands in the air and turn around slowly."

He did as she asked.

She stood there dripping wet.

And very, very naked.

As awe inspiring as that sight was, however, the revolver held steady in her hands, barrel pointed right at the middle of his chest, demanded his full attention.

"You owe me an explanation," she said. "Better make it a good one."

Everything he thought to say died on his lips.

She lowered the gun and in the next instant apparently became aware of her state of undress. "Don't you dare leave," she said scowling and, turning gracefully on bare heels, strode back into the bathroom, banging the door behind her.

Hell, he wouldn't have left for a million dollars.

A belly laugh rolled up his throat and erupted. It died a second later when the bathroom door flew open and Elle reappeared, still frowning, this time wrapped in a towel with her fair hair combed back from her freshly scrubbed and stunning face. She looked impossibly healthy and so alive she burned up the room.

She'd also apparently left the gun in the bathroom.

"What do you think you're doing?" she snapped.

"I thought I was searching your cabin," he said, but it was hard to talk. Somehow, and go figure this one out, she looked more naked with a towel on than she had without it. But maybe that was because the image of her glistening nude body had burned itself into his brain. Her breasts, smaller than he'd thought they would be, but perfectly formed. The smooth skin of her belly. The curves between breasts and hips. Her legs—

His hands almost itched with the desire to stride on over to her and—

And what? Good grief, get a grip. You've seen naked women before.

"Are you always so careless?" she asked, moving toward the closet. She picked up her purse and threw it on the bed, then reached for her robe. Turning her back to him, she pulled it on as the towel puddled around her bare feet. By the time she turned, she was belted into blue terry cloth and much easier to talk to.

"Not usually," he said, lowering his hands.

"Breaking and entering—"

"Your door wasn't locked. Technically, no breaking."

She frowned as though thinking, then perched on the edge of her bed, crossing her legs, studying him.

"Why?"

"Did I toss your place?"

She nodded.

"Because the boss wants you to fly you out with us tomorrow. I had to make sure you are who you said you were."

"He is?"

"Yep. I told you the wet T-shirt was a no-brainer."

"What about the boys in security?"

"They're slow. Must be a backlog."

"And are you satisfied now?"

"Yeah."

"Just from looking through my purse?"

"Just from looking through your purse. Of course, I'm a professional."

A smile broke unexpectedly, curving her lips, lighting her eyes. It transformed her face and he felt a grin tug at the corners of his own lips in response. It was like that sensation he'd had earlier, about there being two Elles behind the eyes.

As the smile fizzled, she said, "Are you worried that I'm the one sending death threats to Alazandro?"

"I hadn't thought of that," he said truthfully. "Of course, up until a few minutes ago, I didn't know you packed a gun."

"I grew up on a ranch."

"Which explains the horse riding and artillery skills."

"That's right."

He tilted his head and stared into her eyes. Now that he knew to look, he could see the tiny curved edges of her contact lenses. He said, "Alazandro was right, Ms. Medina. You are full of surprises."

"Damn right."

"Peg Stiles doesn't want you to leave. She's pretty sure Alazandro is out to corrupt you."

"What do you think?" she asked, pulling the edges of her robe together. They'd fallen apart to reveal a creamy patch of thigh and he took a steadying breath. It wouldn't do to start feeling all sexy towards Alazandro's current conquest-to-be.

He said, "I think Peg is right."

Elle's smile was back, not quite as illuminating. "So do I."

"So, we're back to square one," he said, "although it is odd how cool and calm you are after finding me searching your cabin. Most women wouldn't confront a man stark naked, you know."

"That's true. But you already knew I was a brazen hussy."

"Yeah. But you didn't know it was me when you barged out of the bathroom."

"I didn't *barge*, I crept. Besides, it didn't matter who it was. No one should have been here. Period."

"Do you always take a gun with you when you shower?"

"Not always."

"Wouldn't it be easier to lock your front door?"

"Would that have stopped you?"

"No," he admitted.

"Anyway, why am I explaining myself to you? You're the bad guy, here."

"You need a passport," he said.

"I have one."

He looked around the cabin and said, "Where?"

"None of your business."

"It's in your car, right?"

"I repeat, it's none of your business."

"You know, most women wouldn't sit around in a skimpy robe talking to a virtual stranger, either."

"You look harmless to me," she said.

"Ouch."

"Except for the gun you carry in back under the vest."

"I hardly ever shoot beautiful women," he said, smiling.

"That's reassuring."

He stepped forward and extended a hand, which she took. He pulled her to her feet and then against his chest. She came without resistance. Wiping a wet strand of hair away from her soft cheek, he lowered his voice and said, "I don't know what you're up to, Elle Medina, but you're up to something. I'm going to be watching you."

She didn't even blink. Part of him wanted to rattle her. Was she always this controlled?

"So you're not going to tell Alazandro I'm unsuitable for the job?" she said.

The woman was a one-note song. He had a feeling he could light the curtains on fire and she'd ask about Alazandro and a job while the place burned to the ground around her.

Why?

Narrowing his eyes, he said, "Hell, no, I'm not going to tell him that. From what I've seen, you and he are perfect for one another. If the security boys say you're okay, you're in." And with that, he dipped his head and claimed her mouth.

What had he expected? A slap, a shove, an oath?

She kissed him back, in force, her lips as soft and luscious as he'd known they'd be, her terry-wrapped body a perfect fit against his, her hands gripping his arms, the cleanly washed scent of her enveloping him like perfume.

He told himself he was winning her over to his camp in order to use her. As the kiss grew longer and he felt his soul slipping away, he reminded himself that wars create causalities.

She pushed him away at last, looking a little less composed than she had a few moments earlier.

"I should smack you for that," she said, brown eyes stormy.

"But you won't," he said and, wiping his mouth with the back of his hand, swaggered out of her cabin like an actor in a B-grade movie.

Chapter Three

After her last lesson, Elle helped Mike groom and bed down the horses. She'd miss Mike, she realized, and she'd miss the horses. As careful as she'd been to avoid putting down any roots while biding time at Tahoe Stables, roots had grown all on their own. She'd even miss Peg.

Elle finished wiping down Majordomo's back, the bay gelding dancing around even more than usual. Maybe he sensed her mood. More spirited than Corky, he made a more interesting mount for an able rider. He looked at her over his shoulder and she patted his white blaze, crooning to him a little. Then she unhooked his lead from the post and led him to his stall.

"I want you to have my car," she told Mike as she unhooked the lead from Majordomo's halter and closed the stall door. "I have to use it tonight but, after that, it's all yours."

Mike looked up from pouring oats into Corky's feed bag. "Your car? I can't—"

"Sure you can," she said. "It leaks oil like a sieve and needs new tires. Half the time it won't start. It's not that big a deal."

"But you'll need it when you come back from Puerta

Del Sol," Mike said, replacing the lid on the barrel they used to store grain.

"How do you know about that?"

"The big blond guy told me. He was asking questions about you." Mike cast her a grin and added, "Don't worry, I told him I'd never seen you fall off a horse before today."

She hung the lead from a nail as she said, "Thanks. Well, anyway, I'm not coming back." Her voice sounded serene. She was a good actress.

For a second, it seemed she might never be herself again.

But that was stupid. The trouble was she was too much herself. She couldn't seem to stop responding to things. To Peg's disappointment in her, to news of the judge's arrival, and lordy, lordy, to Pete.

He made her feel she was on fire inside.

First the verbal teasing, which she'd enjoyed, then that kiss. A man like that didn't kiss a woman for the hell of it, he'd been prying into her life with that kiss and she'd let him.

And she'd enjoyed it.

She smiled to herself. The naked part hadn't been planned, but it sure had caught his attention. She'd gotten out of the shower, heard a noise, grabbed the gun from the cabinet behind the sink and entered the room without hesitation. Along with her passport, she hid papers under a loose floorboard. Papers about her family's murders, about the suspects, about Alazandro.

The expression on his handsome face when he turned around had been priceless. And admit it, she'd enjoyed the sensations his strong body pressed against hers had aroused. His lips, the flicker of his tongue.

The flames leaped.

She reminded herself of her goal: get close to Alazandro. And then she added a new goal: keep away from Pete.

"That's a cool job," Mike mused. "You must be real excited about it."

She nodded and smiled. She *was* kind of excited, which was dumb. She wasn't going there to play with the horses and make a great stable. She was going to discover the truth about Víctor Alazandro and bring him to justice—dead or alive.

That sobering thought wiped the memory of Pete's playful banter and kiss right out of her thoughts.

Mike grabbed the broom from against a wall and started sweeping the walkway. As he rambled on about his plans for the future, uncomplicated plans Elle envied, she decided she had to get Peg to understand that Mike deserved a chance. He and Peg would make a good team. Peg's savvy, Mike's personality. They could make a go of whatever remained after Alazandro got finished with them.

Wait, an additional goal: ruin Alazandro before he could ruin Peg.

"Who's going to take over the riding lessons here?" Mike asked.

Elle blinked a couple of times. She'd been lost in her thoughts. How to answer? She didn't want to raise any false hopes—

The answer came from behind Elle. "You are, Mike," Peg said as she entered the stable.

"But I have to tend the horses," Mike said, leaning on the broom. "I have to exercise and—"

"Starting tomorrow, you do everything Elle did. We've already got Pam and Tracy coming in to help with mucking out stables and exercising. I'll get the Hoskins boy to do your chores until we can find someone more permanent. Get some sleep tonight, you're going to have a big day tomorrow."

With that, she nodded at Mike and left the stable.

"What's with her?" Mike whispered to Elle. "She didn't even look at you."

"She's got a lot on her mind," Elle said.

Mike nodded and then grinned. "I wonder if she'll let me move into your cabin. It's bigger than mine."

"You're kidding."

"Nope. I have to use the outhouse."

Elle laughed. "You're moving up in the world, my friend."

"Yeah," he said. "Thanks to you and Mr. Alazandro."

A HALF HOUR LATER, Elle was in her car, trying in vain to get the motor to turn over. The oil light shone red, which meant she'd neglected to add oil the last time she used the car. Great, she was probably willing Mike a car with a cracked head. On the other hand, he was getting a practically new *Learn Japanese in Thirty Days* tape, which was still stuck in the car's tape player.

Someone rapped on her window.

She cranked it down to find Pete leaning down, peering in at her.

"Trouble?" he said.

"No."

"Are you sure?"

Shrugging, she made a decision. Fate had taken a hand, she wouldn't drive into town.

Meeting with the judge would be a waste of time, anyway. She could hear his arguments in her head. *The dean owes me one, I know I can get you back into*

graduate school. Your grandfather is caught up in sense-
less vengeance and neither you nor that nurse of his is
helping. Don't buy into it. Leave the past alone, don't risk
your future, what's done is done, nothing will bring your
dead family back to life. Justice will be done in the end.

If he had any inkling she was flying out with Alazandro tomorrow morning, he'd kill her. Or Alazandro.

"Elle?"

She got out of the car and leaned against the door. After
a moment or two, Pete joined her, his body too close for
comfort. She contemplated moving and decided it would
send the wrong message. Or the right one.

Face it, she found his presence disconcerting. The man
exuded confidence from the ends of his short sandy hair
to the tips of his worn boots. Add the physique, the eyes,
the rugged features, the voice—

When he looked at her, a private spot inside melted.

Life was confusing enough without him. Why did he
have to come along now, why did he have to be connected to Alazandro? And why couldn't she walk away
from him without looking back?

"Going to be a beautiful evening," he said.

Lake Tahoe lay down the sloping property, a glittering
jewel this late in the day, a beautiful blue gem caught in
the palm of towering trees.

"You seem upset," Pete added.

"A little."

"I came out here this evening to deliver some papers
to Peg Stiles. She seems upset, too."

Elle cast him a quick glance. Her gaze landed on his
lips and she quickly raised her eyes. He smiled down at
her.

Damn him.

She said, "As a matter of fact, I'm annoyed with my adopted father, not Peg. How about you, Pete? Do you have a father? Or a last name? Or a dog? Anything?"

It took him a moment to answer. She could almost feel his thoughts spinning. "Yes to the first two, no to the third. Father alive and kicking in Maui with his fourth wife. My last name is Waters."

"Peter Waters." She wasn't sure she believed him, though why he should lie was a mystery. Maybe he had a record or something. Maybe instead of being a cop in his former life he'd been a felon.

He apparently wasn't finished prying. "So, what did this adopted father do to upset you?"

"For most my life, showed me nothing but kindness," Elle said in a burst of truth.

"The cad."

She laughed softly.

"But lately?"

"Lately he's been—unreasonable."

"With you? That's hard to understand."

She heard the smile in his voice. "I haven't always been this easygoing," she said.

"Now that's hard to believe."

"Yeah, right." In another burst of candor, she added, "I wasn't an easy child to bring up. I had nightmares. My family had all died in an...accident...and I was left alone. The judge was my father's best friend. They worked together on the police force. They had set it up to take care of each other's children if something happened to one of them. But the judge didn't have any children of his own and a year after he and his wife adopted me, she died, so he got the full burden of trying to take care of a bereft little girl."

Pete started to speak but didn't. She was relieved, afraid that if he offered a sympathetic shoulder to cry on, she'd take him up on it. "Anyway, now he just wants me to go back to school and become a professor and make him proud."

"While your life's ambition is to work at a resort for Víctor Alazandro."

"Does that mean I got a go-ahead from Mr. Alazandro's security people?"

"That's what it means. You fly out with us tomorrow."

She bit back a smile and a shudder, both of which were spontaneous responses to the same stimuli. "Where is Mr. Alazandro, anyway?"

"He's having dinner at one of the casinos with an investor."

"Who's watching his back?"

"Night shift."

She pushed herself away from the car. "I have to find a phone and call the judge to tell him I'm not coming. See you tomorrow."

"We'll pick you up at six. But wait a minute." He caught her hand and pulled her gently back to stand in front of him, a battle waging behind his eyes. Ignoring the warmth radiating up her arm from contact with his hand, she waited.

Taking a deep breath, he said, "If you tell Alazandro I told you this, I swear I'll shoot you."

She stopped breathing. "Tell him what?"

He narrowed his eyes. "Don't come with us tomorrow. Stay here. Go back where you came from. Just don't come to Puerta Del Sol."

"Don't you start this, too," she said with a sigh.

"I know you want to get close to Alazandro."

"What?"

"He's a rich, important guy. You've had a hard life and your adopted father is bugging you. Flying off to Mexico must sound exciting—"

She started to laugh again, but stopped. "You're not joking, are you?"

He lowered his head until his breath felt warm against her face, intoxicating and frightening at the same time. Whispering, he said, "No, I'm not joking. He's a dangerous man."

"Like you?"

He swore under his breath as he released her hand. "You are the singular most irritating woman I've ever known and that's saying something."

"But I thought the danger came from outside."

"What do you mean?"

"From whoever issued the death threat against him."

Pete nodded solemnly. "Yeah, that's right."

"But now you're telling me it's Alazandro himself I need protecting from?"

He glared at her.

"You need to get your story straight," she said brightly.

"The last time we were down there, a young woman died of a drug overdose."

"That's terrible, but how does that—"

"She was alone with Alazandro at the time. Alazandro was questioned. He claimed no knowledge of what happened."

"Are you implying Mr. Alazandro killed her?"

Pete looked away, then back. "No."

"That he gave her illegal drugs?"

"No."

"Okay, then listen to me. I *have* to go to Puerta Del Sol.

I want to go." And with that she took off, anxious to get away from him before he could lure her back. She knew what kind of man Alazandro was, so why did Pete's warning, if it was a warning and not some bizarre test, send the granddaddy of shivers racing down her spine?

AFTER A RESTLESS NIGHT spent wrestling the blankets, Elle was up and dressed early.

She'd had the nightmare again last night. Her father, facedown on the floor. Her standing at the top of the stairs. Her crying out, him turning, his face dissolving into a pulpy, bloody mess as he got to his feet, his flesh slipping from his rotting corpse as he started up the stairs toward her.

Always the same dream, not as often now as before, but always the same. She'd finally told her grandfather about it and he'd shaken his white head. "Janey, it's clear to me your father wants justice for himself, for your mother and for your baby brother," he'd said. He'd continued calling her Janey despite the judge's protests. "I've been thinking about this ever since I was diagnosed with this blasted cancer. I shouldn't have allowed their deaths to go unavenged and now it's too late. Unless—"

That conversation had set everything else in motion and had strangely almost ended the dream, as though her father knew she was committed to avenge them all.

And now she was finally on the brink of making good on that promise.

The conversation with the judge the night before had been horrific. He'd demanded she return with him, she'd refused. He'd called her spoiled, she'd called him controlling. They'd finally agreed to meet for lunch, a promise she'd known she couldn't keep. She'd be long gone by then. She felt wretched lying to him. Justified, but wretched.

She didn't know what game Pete was playing or even if he was playing a game, but she knew she couldn't afford to take the papers about her family's deaths with her to Mexico. Pete seemed to have a penchant for spontaneous searches and every document she carried was way too incriminating.

Leaving the pink slip and the car keys on the table for Mike, she left her cabin at the first sign of daylight. She carried her purse strapped across her chest along with her duffel bag, packed with her clothes and the gun as well as a box of ammunition. It wasn't chilly enough to wear both jackets, but she did so anyway as they wouldn't fit in the duffel and she needed to have her hands empty.

The burn pile was located beside the hay barn and she made her way to it over uneven, dew-soaked grass. The papers went up in a cheery little blaze that did nothing to cheer her. The enormity of what she'd set in motion the day before had begun to sink in, creating a dandy case of performance anxiety.

She would have to flirt her way south today. She'd have to keep up the sexy, provocative persona whenever Alazandro was around. Playful, but not too easy because the goal was to avoid sleeping with him.

She heard approaching footsteps and turned to find Peg wearing a loose Windbreaker over jeans, a jacket Elle had never seen before. Peg's face looked drawn as though she, too, hadn't slept much.

"I saw the open flame," she said, pulling the collar up around her throat with one hand as she raised a cigarette to her lips with the other.

"I had some old love letters to get rid of," Elle lied.

Peg nodded as she flipped the cigarette into the last of the blaze. She exhaled a breath of smoke that mingled with the campfire's. The two women stood there for a few seconds as the blaze flickered and died. Then they both started to speak at once. Elle said, "Go ahead, please."

Peg glanced at Elle's face, then away. "I was out of line yesterday," she finally said as though each word took effort.

"Peg—"

"No, listen. I made a mistake getting involved with Alazandro. It was before I hired you, right after my husband died. I was broke. The mortgage we'd taken to see Bill through his illness—well, anyway, Alazandro somehow heard about my problems and swept in here like a conquering hero. He promised me I could keep everything as it was. He promised me the moon. My lawyer warned me but I couldn't see any other way out. I signed papers and now—well, now it's too late."

Peg's voice had softened to a whisper as she tucked both hands in her pockets and stared at the smoldering ashes. One side of her jacket hung lower than the other and obviously held a heavy cylindrical object like a flashlight. The thought of Peg wandering around her beloved property in the dark dressed in what looked like her late husband's old coat made Elle's throat swell.

Peg added, "But that has nothing to do with you. I shouldn't have done what I did."

"You didn't *do* anything, Peg. You just expressed your opinions and—"

"I called your father."

Elle closed her eyes and rocked back on her heels.

"I was just so blasted mad! Víctor Alazandro is one of

those people who destroy everything and everybody they touch."

Elle took a steadying breath. The judge wasn't home, he was here, in Nevada, Peg couldn't have talked to him. It was okay.

Peg said, "Mike told me your father was staying at the Lakefront Inn. So I called his room early this morning. Woke him up, but I had to do something. I told him you were leaving this morning with Alazandro. He said something about over his dead body and hung up the phone and then I saw you down here and I know I should have minded my own business, but it's too late now. I wanted to tell you about this myself. Before he got here and—"

Elle grabbed Peg's arm. "The judge is coming here?"

Peg nodded miserably. "There's only one way out of this mess," she said. "It's up to me."

Elle didn't know or care much what Peg meant by that. She grabbed her duffel bag and took off toward the dirt parking area located by the largest stable. That's where Pete and Alazandro would arrive. She glanced at her watch. It was almost six.

What would the judge do?

Threaten her? Threaten Alazandro? Would he say something that would alarm Alazandro enough to make him back out of taking her to Puerta Del Sol with him?

Of course he would.

She glanced back to ask how long ago Peg had talked to the judge. It took twenty minutes to drive here from town and if he'd been asleep, he would have had to dress—

Peg was nowhere in sight.

Elle scanned the area around the hay barn until a movement twenty feet above the ground at the opening used for loading feed drew her attention. Peg stood in the shadows, the flashlight in her hand.

Elle turned away and took a few more steps before realizing what she'd seen wasn't a flashlight.

Peg was holding a gun. Most likely the .357 Magnum her husband had kept in the gun case located behind his big oak desk. Peg had bragged about him teaching her to shoot it….

At that moment, Elle heard a car on the gravel road and spun around to find a sleek sedan pulling into the parking area, Pete behind the wheel, Alazandro beside him in the passenger seat.

She ran as fast as she could, determined to get to the car before either man got out. She was closest to Alazandro's side.

As the thinning verge turned to dirt, Elle skidded on the last of the dewy grass, landing on her knees, the duffel bag jarred from her hand. Pete and Alazandro opened their respective doors.

She looked up to see both men staring at her. Before she could utter a word, sunlight glinted off something on the hillside opposite the barn, behind the car. Narrowing her eyes, Elle saw the long barrel of a rifle. Behind it loomed a red truck.

The judge drove a big four-wheel-drive Dodge Ram, candy apple red. Gun rack in back. Vintage Winchester .401 caliber autoloading deer rifle always at hand….

She screamed a warning and ducked her head as a shot rang out and a bit of earth at Elle's knee exploded. Covering her head with her arms, she saw Alazandro dive back into the car as more shots seemed to come from every direction. Pete was suddenly at her side, grabbing her arm, yanking her to her feet. She lunged toward her duffel bag until another shot took a bite out of the ground an inch from her boot.

To hell with the duffel bag.

She ran ahead of Pete who seemed to be one step ahead of gunfire. The driver's door stood ajar. Pete all but threw her inside where she quickly climbed between the seats into the back, aware of Alazandro sitting crumpled with his head against the dashboard. Pete climbed in after her. The gun still clutched in his hand, he started the car, revved the engine and turned the wheel sharply to take off back down the gravel road.

Gasping for breath, Elle looked out the rear window.

Which one of them, Peg or the judge, had just attempted to murder Víctor Alazandro?

And as she looked at Alazandro's slumped figure, a new thought surfaced.

Had they succeeded?

Chapter Four

What the hell was going on?

Pete glanced in the rearview mirror. His gaze collided with Elle's. Wide brown eyes met his gaze and shied away.

"Are you okay?" he demanded.

She nodded.

She'd been worried that standing too close to Alazandro might be dangerous and she'd been right.

As far as Pete knew, there had never been a death threat made against Víctor Alazandro. That piece of fiction had been created by the DEA right before the staged shoot-out during which Pete had rescued Alazandro from a crazed gunman. Agent Ben Kipper had made a very believable, wigged-out drug addict firing blanks at Alazandro until Pete had single-handedly subdued him.

Alazandro hired him on the spot.

Still, Pete could understand someone taking shots at Alazandro. Peg Stiles came readily to mind. But would Peg shoot at Elle? No way.

That left Elle's adopted father who Elle had told him was in the area last night. That meant the man had to love her enough to come to Tahoe to try and talk to her about something she obviously didn't want to talk to him about, but hate her enough to take potshots at her when she blew him off.

Again, no way, it didn't add up.

Someone had tried to kill Alazandro and hadn't cared a whole lot who else they hit.

What was needed, of course, was a crime scene investigation. Collection of spent shells. Bullet trajectories. Witness interviews. All of that was as good as lost because Pete couldn't break cover to call in the cops.

As he steered the car onto the main highway, he darted a quick look at Alazandro. Blood trickled down his forehead, ran along his cheek. "Sir?" Pete said, almost choking on the word.

Without looking up, Alazandro responded in a shaky voice. "Is it safe now?"

"Yeah," Pete said. "You've been hit," he added.

Alazandro's voice was shaky as he mumbled, "I bashed my head when you shoved me into the car. It's my arm that hurts like hell." He turned in his seat. His left hand clutched the sleeve of his right arm. Blood soaked the tattered cloth between his fingers. The suit was history.

Following a gasp, Elle said, "The hospital is about fifteen minutes away. Take a right when you get to the second intersection—"

In unison, Pete and Alazandro said, "No!"

She was quiet for a second before trying again. "You need a doctor, Mr. Alazandro."

"Doctors have to report gunshot wounds to the cops," Pete said.

A longer silence was followed by a tentative, "But aren't we going to tell the police what happened?"

Alazandro said, "No hospital and no police, Ms. Medina. I'm a busy man and don't intend on getting stuck stateside in some worthless investigation when I have a jet waiting. Pete, get us to the airport. You know first aid, you can patch me up after we're in the air."

Pete drove. Another glimpse in the rearview mirror revealed Elle shrugging off her bulky jacket and the denim one she wore beneath. "You'd better use this to stop the blood from getting all over the upholstery," she said, handing the denim jacket over the car seat to Alazandro.

He pressed it against his arm and smiled back at her.

"You're very brave," she cooed, sitting forward and touching his good shoulder.

Alazandro kind of puffed out his chest and sighed.

Wait a second. Shouldn't Elle Medina be shaking like a leaf, shouldn't she be demanding to be let off at the nearest police department? The woman had nerves of steel.

As enticing a potential spy as she might make, however, Pete couldn't put her in harm's way. He needed to find a way to make a surreptitious call and arrange an incident at the airport that would prevent Elle from boarding Alazandro's private jet. A fake customs ploy, maybe. A phony arrest warrant—

Alazandro said, "Whoever is trying to get me came damn close this time."

Pete said, "He came close to getting all three of us."

Elle whistled. "You can say that again."

Pete, sensing his chance, said, "We don't need someone else to worry about, boss. Leave the woman here. She can fly down later."

As Alazandro glanced into the back seat, Pete used the

mirror. Elle's blinding white T-shirt revealed an amazing amount of creamy cleavage. The top curves of her breasts looked smooth and inviting. The stirring in Pete's groin had as much to do with the memory of her naked as it did with her wavering image in the mirror. She flicked a few blond hairs away from her heart-shaped face and smiled, eyes crinkling at the edges as she licked her lips for Alazandro.

The temptress was back.

Pete said, "We had to leave your duffel bag back at the stable. It probably held your passport—"

"Nope, that's right here in my purse."

"Stop fussing, you're not her father," Alazandro said, casting Pete an annoyed frown. He added, "I hear your father is a judge, Elle. Whereabouts?"

"Down in Butter Gulch, Arizona," she said.

"I built a resort down that way a few years ago," he said, wincing as he tried to get comfortable. "Near the border. So you grew up in Arizona?"

"No. I was born in Seattle, Washington. I didn't move to Arizona until after my parents died when I was five."

Alazandro peered into the back seat again. "Then your father isn't really your father—"

"Adopted. He worked with my dad. He and his wife took me in. We all moved to Arizona a few weeks later."

"I used to live in Seattle," Alazandro said.

There was a slight pause before she said, "Really? When?"

"A long time ago. I was a kid."

"I bet you were a handful," Elle said, her voice as silky as satin sheets.

He laughed. "I had my moments."

Her next question came slowly. "Why did you leave?"

He shrugged his uninjured shoulder. "There was some trouble. The cops thought I was involved. I decided it was time to start over. I had family in San Diego and big ambitions, so I moved down there."

Elle's face, reflected in Pete's mirror, had turned to stone.

"The rest is history," Alazandro added.

Elle surprised Pete by saying, "How about Mr. Waters here? How did you two meet up?"

Alazandro laughed. "Pete saved my life a few months back. Stepped right into the middle of a mess. He didn't even work for me. I rectified that, of course. Made him an offer he couldn't refuse."

"Good thinking," Elle cooed.

"He almost took a bullet for me," Alazandro mused in an awed voice.

"You're lucky to have him," Elle said.

Alazandro snorted. "I pay him well. Money buys loyalty, Ms. Medina. The minute that loyalty wavers, I cut my losses. Permanently. Remember that."

Pete chanced one more glance in the mirror and caught Elle staring at the back of Alazandro's head.

She was back to asking a lot of questions, this time of Alazandro himself. What was she hiding behind those pretty brown eyes?

Pete made a decision. He wouldn't stand in the way of her coming with them. He wouldn't fake some situation that kept her grounded. Until he knew just what she was up to, he'd keep her close by.

He told himself it had to do with the bigger picture but inside the truth elbowed his conscience. He wanted her nearby for two reasons. One, he didn't trust her. She was up to something and he was duty bound to make sure it

didn't impact his own mission. Two, for some unex-
plainable reason, he was worried about her. Not the
version currently sitting in the back seat, but the one
buried inside, the one who peeked out now and again, the
one who had survived a volley of bullets.

This time.

How had she gotten under his skin so fast and what was
he going to do about it?

ELLE LICKED DRY LIPS. Alazandro had left Seattle after
running into trouble. She knew this, of course. He'd been
involved with drugs when he was young. Maybe he'd
been whacked out of his mind when he slew her family.

What startled her now was the way he'd admitted
leaving. Without hesitation. Like it was nothing. Like it
was a parking violation or a speeding ticket and not the
wholesale slaughter of a man, woman and infant.

She squeezed her eyes shut for a moment, her mind
jumping from one wild set of thoughts to another. From
the fact Alazandro and Pete had both left the shooting at
the stable unreported to the burning question—who had
fired those shots?

The judge? A man who had dedicated his life to the
law? Straight arrow Daniel Medina jeopardizing his
career because of a homicidal whim? Because of her?

Or Peg Stiles. Peg was certainly hotheaded enough.
But she'd been toting a handgun and been quite a distance
away. Who was to say a different weapon hadn't been
stored in the hay loft hours before, though?

Or had both of them fired?

Alazandro's playful mood quickly vanished as the pain
from his gunshot was compounded by irritation when
they got to the airport only to discover the copilot was

late. Under Pete's baleful glare, Elle sat next to Alazandro in the small waiting area, her gaze returning over and over again to the wall phone. She was dying to call the stable and make sure everyone was okay. Every time she decided she would, she caught Pete's eye. She didn't want him thinking about that shooting. She didn't want him getting the judge or Peg in trouble. So she sat where she was and watched her favorite denim jacket turn brown with Alazandro's dried blood.

The copilot finally arrived, a man with thick auburn hair and hazel eyes that slid to Alazandro and away as he apologized. Elle wondered how much longer the poor guy would have a job.

During the first leg of the flight, Pete cut away what was left of Alazandro's shirt and cleaned and bandaged the older man's arm. His touch was sure, his movements deft, and as she held bandages and averted her gaze from the bloody mess, she found herself mesmerized by the skilled way Pete took charge.

What kind of lover would he make? Cool and competent like he was now? Or hot and dangerous as he'd been the day before when he kissed her?

After landing in Ensenada to clear customs and refuel, they continued on to Puerta Del Sol. Alazandro fell asleep with his head resting against Elle's collarbone, his hot breath tunneling down her cleavage. It was all Elle could do to allow—no, to encourage—the contact when all she really wanted was to push him away in disgust and demand details about why he'd left Seattle.

Pete, staring at her with his upper lip lifted in contempt, didn't help matters. Damn him. Why did he have to watch her all the time? Why did he have to look so disappointed in her? And why did she care what he thought about her or anything else?

Once they made the final landing, Alazandro woke looking a little glassy eyed. He waved away Pete's offer of help, instead leaning against Elle as they disembarked.

A white limousine pulled up to the stopped plane and Pete shuffled Alazandro inside as his gaze scanned the desert-like landscape.

"Looking for something?" Elle asked, half in and half out of the limo. It was hot and muggy and she wiped her forearm against her brow.

"Just the usual," he said.

She followed his gaze as it swept sandy earth, low-lying bushes and some mountains off to the east. Only a few large aluminum buildings on the other side of the airstrip provided cover. Touching Pete's arm, she pointed that way.

"Those warehouses? Not likely," he said. "They're relatively new, built along with the landing strip specifically for this place. No handy trees or bushes to hide behind, damn few windows."

"What airlines fly in here?" she asked. There didn't seem to be a tower or a passenger area that she could see.

"There are no commercial flights in or out. There's a highway to the east, but it's bumpy and dusty so most everything gets flown in. There is no real town of Puerta Del Sol, the resort sits off by itself on the bluff. The closest town is Las Brisas."

"Is that where the people who run the airport live?"

"Some of them. The pilots stay at up the resort during layovers."

"Should we wait for them?"

He lowered his voice. "Are you kidding? Alazandro

share a car with what he calls a fancy bus driver? No, they'll take care of themselves."

The road leading away from the airstrip was smooth and well maintained. As they neared the resort, the environment became landscaped, with pastures on either side of the road, each surrounded with bright white fencing and dotted with horses. Even Alazandro came out of his funk and sighed with pleasure as two chestnuts tossed their heads and trotted alongside the fence.

Both horses appeared to be top quality Arabs, their healthy coats glistening in the sunshine, their confirmation impeccable. A few other horses, grazing on remarkably green grass, looked of decent breeding but past their prime.

"There's quite a difference in horses," she said.

"You mean in the quality," Alazandro said. "The pasture on the right is used as a kind of holding pen for animals in transit from down south to a dude ranch located far north of here at a place outside of Agua Prieta."

"That's across the border from the Arizona city of Douglas, isn't it? I didn't know you had a dude ranch."

"I don't. It belongs to a business associate of mine. I'm doing him a favor."

"That's very kind of you," she gushed.

"Kindness has nothing to do with it," he said, sparing her the kind of tolerant smile a parent gives an amusing child.

The road led past a beautiful adobe and wood stable before continuing onto a broad headland on which the resort itself had been built. A succession of sprawling single story structures was backed by the glistening blue expanse of the Pacific Ocean. Palm trees, winding paths and colorful flowers set off white stucco walls and red tile roofs.

The car rolled to a stop at the base of wide steps leading to a generous patio. Workmen on ladders applied the last tiles of an elaborate mosaic depicting a rising sun with spreading rays of gold against a lapis background. The sun mosaic encircled an arched doorway that emptied into the shady lobby beyond. The words *Puerta Del Sol* had been set in tiles above the door. Curved branches of brilliant pink, purple and coral bougainvillea added a final riot of color.

Pete got out and opened Elle's door. She looked back at Alazandro who raised her hand to his lips. "I have private quarters around the back," he said.

"You should see a doctor," she cautioned.

"There's one waiting in my quarters. But first, I have business to attend to. Come see me late this evening. We'll have a midnight supper. Pete will show you the way."

"What about my job—"

"Someone will fill you in," he said, his tone dismissing her.

For a second, Elle wondered what would happen if she jumped on his lap and planted a big old wet kiss on his plump lips. She had to think of some way of getting better access to him than midnight suppers.

But he'd looked away as though she'd ceased to exist. She climbed out of the car into the sweltering heat. Only the whisper of a breeze blowing off the ocean made it tolerable. Female voices came from inside the lobby.

Pete's gaze searched the surrounding buildings as he said, "The employee housing isn't ready for occupation yet, so you'll stay in the resort. Wait indoors for me."

"Why?"

"Just do. I'll be back as soon as I can." Pinning her with his blue eyes, he added, "I assume your gun was inside the duffel bag that got left behind."

"Why would you assume that?"

He gave the sleeveless, tight white shirt and the jeans she'd wiggled into that morning a lingering once-over. "There's no place in your clothes to hide a weapon."

Elle jiggled the coat she carried looped through her arm. She'd left the blood stained denim jacket in the airport back in Tahoe. "How do you know it's not buried deep in a pocket?"

"I looked. Be careful."

"Are you determined to scare me every chance you get?"

It took him a second to respond and when he did it was like the words had to fight their way out into the open. "That shooting seemed to come out of the blue."

"Isn't *surprise* the modus operandi of an assassin?"

He stared right into her eyes. His voice when he spoke sounded wary. "Maybe."

What did he mean by that? Was he on to the judge or Peg? She said, "Maybe whoever was behind that shooting was trying to take you out."

"Sure," he said.

"You couldn't really blame them," she said.

He flashed a sudden smile at her. "That's not nice."

"It's just that you're so annoying—"

He slapped a hand against his chest. "I'm annoying? Ha!" With that he pushed her toward the arched doorway.

As the limo disappeared around the far right building, Elle took sanctuary inside the lobby, squeezing past a cluster of very young women who regarded her with curiosity. The lobby looked all but finished, mosaic covering many of the walls, including those leading off to restaurants and shops that hadn't opened yet.

Mumbling, *"Excusa,"* she finally caught the eye of a harried looking middle-aged woman with long dark hair wound atop her head. *"¿Senora?"* Elle called. *"¿Telefono por favor?"*

A name tag pinned to her ample bosom read "Linda Gonzales. Head of Household Management." Her laugh was infectious. "No need for Spanish, hon, I was born and raised in Texas. You must be Elle Medina. We're interviewing maids today but Mr. Alazandro's office called ahead and said you'd be coming. I have a room ready for you."

Impressed with the efficiency of Alazandro's organization, Elle said, "I need a phone—"

Linda Gonzales dug in her apron pocket. "Calling the States?" she said, handing Elle a cell phone. "Use this one, it's easier than trying to dial out. You can borrow it until you get one of your own." She looked behind Elle and added, "Is someone bringing your luggage?"

"I'm traveling light," Elle said.

AS LUNCH ON THE PLANE seemed to have come and gone a week before and dinner was apparently to be a midnight affair, Elle snacked on the fruit basket she found in her suite. The place was drop-dead gorgeous.

Her grandfather answered his cell on the first ring. His voice, which always sounded weak to Elle, sounded even more frail and a lump the size of a papaya lodged in her throat.

But he had news and after admitting he was too breathless to impart it himself, handed the phone to Scott.

"So what's going on?" Elle asked.

"My brother, the police detective, looked at the evidence they still have up in Seattle," Scott said with his usual humor. "There's not much."

"I know. Most of it disappeared, right?"

"Yeah. There's an old cassette tape, but no handy fingerprints and no way to know whose voices are recorded. It sounds like a drug deal going down. There was an envelope, but that disappeared. It was rumored to have Alazandro's fingerprints on it, but that information disappeared as well."

"So they have a useless tape?"

"Pretty much." Elle heard her grandfather's soft voice in the background. Scott obviously covered the receiver. She heard a muffled, "I'll tell her."

"Tell me what?"

"My brother found a retired detective who worked on the case. He's talking to him tomorrow. I can't see what he can tell Kevin, but it's got your grandpa all psyched."

"If there's anything I should know—"

"I'll call."

She gave him the cell phone number and warned him she didn't know how long she'd have it so to be circumspect if he did call. She added, "Is Grandpa doing as bad as he sounds?"

Scott's voice was entirely too hearty as he said, "He's doing great."

Elle talked for a moment or two to her grandfather, but it was pretty clear his stamina was spent and they hung up soon after.

The judge didn't answer his cell phone. He hadn't had time to drive home yet so that meant he was probably on the road and he'd probably forgotten to turn his phone on.

A fond smile curved her lips as she thought of him. She'd spent a lifetime wishing they could be closer, but the truth was there had always been something between them and Elle suspected that something was the way her family died. It's hard to build the future on such debris-laden ground.

She tried calling Peg's house and got the answering machine. She then tried the stable and after a dozen rings, a breathless Mike picked up and mumbled, "Tahoe Stables."

"Hey, Mike. It's me, Elle."

"Man, Elle, we've been worried about you," Mike said as Elle paced in and out the open French doors. The Pacific Ocean, far below, rolled endlessly to the horizon. The breeze was fresher out this far on the headland and Elle had turned off the air conditioning and opened all windows and doors to take advantage of it.

"What do you mean?"

"I mean what happened this morning when you were leaving. It was like a war zone."

Elle stopped pacing and stared into the mirror. Her image reflected the stillness in her heart as she said, "Was anyone hurt?"

"That's what we were wondering about you. Your dad says trouble follows Mr. Alazandro around like—"

"Wait, my father is there? The judge is there?"

"Oh yeah, and he's madder than hell. So is Peg."

"And neither one of them knows what happened?"

"Nope. They blame all of it on Mr. Alazandro and that hired gun of his. Your father thought you'd been kidnapped because your duffel bag is still here."

Elle couldn't believe what she was hearing. If the judge had been up on that hill looking through the rifle sight, he knew damn good and well what happened. She said, "I just dropped my bag, that's all and then the gunfire got everyone spooked so we took off in a hurry. So, what did the police say?"

"Your dad said it was pointless calling the cops. He said the danger passed as soon as Mr. Alazandro and his hired gun left."

Mike apparently didn't see the holes in the judge's stated reasoning. If he thought Elle had been kidnapped, he'd have called in the FBI by now. He knew she was safe, he'd seen her get in the car under her own steam.

"Maybe I should talk to him," she said, wondering what on earth she would say.

"He and Peg drove into town for a late lunch."

Who was covering for who? She finally said, "So everything is just…fine?"

"Yeah. Well, Tabitha is driving me nuts, but what's new?"

Elle took a deep breath as a knock sounded on the door. She said goodbye to Mike as she set the cell phone on the nightstand.

Pete looked over her shoulder as he she opened the door. "I thought I heard you talking to someone."

"I called the stable to let them know I made it here safely."

"What did they make of all the excitement this morning?" he asked.

"They decided it was all Alazandro's fault. And yours."

"Smart people." He looked her up and down and added, "I imagine there are things you need, like a change of clothes, maybe."

She glanced down at her white shirt and jeans, the boots on her feet. "A toothbrush would be nice."

"And a nightgown," he said with a sly smile.

"I sleep nude," she replied with an upward glance and a burning desire to rattle him for a change.

"You forget I searched your cabin back in Tahoe," he said. "You wear a little white gown. Though I'd better tell you Alazandro is more of a black lace kind of guy."

She raised her hand to slap him. He caught her wrist, lowering her arm until it rested on top of her head. "Just kidding," he said, but he didn't release her wrist. Instead he dipped his head until his breath felt warm on her forehead.

"You haven't thanked me yet for saving your life back at the stables," he murmured, staring at her lips.

The memory of his lips pressed against hers suddenly occupied every traitorous corner of her mind.

"I risked body and limb to whisk you to safety," he added. "The least I deserve is a thanks."

Her body was going soft in all the right—or rather, wrong—places. She moved back a step but that just pushed her up against the open door and he was still there, his face still just a whisper away.

Releasing his grip on her, his fingers grazed her cheek, sent shivers north and south at hyper speed. His hat was gone, probably knocked off when he'd grabbed her wrist. His eyes traveled her face as though he was looking for something, as though he was memorizing her features for future reference. He whispered, "I'll save you the trouble. You are most welcome."

He was testing her. He was taunting her. He was— kissing her.

As she'd stood there trying to decide how to deal with her mounting libido, he'd lowered his lips the last iota of an inch. The kiss was explosive, shaking her so deep inside it was like a volcano erupting, pouring hot lava into every sexual organ she possessed. He coaxed her lips open and twisted his tongue around hers, probing her mouth, gently splitting her legs apart with his knee as he pressed her against the wooden panel, his lean, hard body inseparable from hers, their clothes all but smoking as their collected heat flared.

She twisted her head away as his hands roamed down her torso, cupped her denim-clad rear. Her breasts pressed tight against him, his growing arousal was hard against her belly. She dug her hands into his back—

"No," she whispered into his ear.

It took him a moment to move fractionally away. She felt his breath again, hot now as he kissed her lips a dozen times, this time without the invasion.

He sighed deeply as he finally unpinned her, leaning his weight on the hand he'd propped beside her head. His stare was as intense as the kiss and she looked away, not trusting herself—not with him.

"Why are you coming on to Alazandro when you feel this way about me?" he asked, his voice different than usual.

His question stunned her. A denial raced through her mind; a flirty nonanswer followed on its heels. She mingled the truth with subterfuge as she finally said, "He…has something I want."

"So do I," Pete said, kissing her forehead a half dozen times, his lips warm and moist.

She closed her eyes and said, "Not like that."

"Not like what?" he asked, his hands cradling her head as his lips touched her eyelids, cheeks, ears. "It's his money, isn't it? Or his power. Admit it."

She drew away from his seductive kisses.

He stared at her a long moment.

She finally whispered, "It's…complicated."

Slowly bending over to retrieve his hat, he produced a half smile. "Okay, Elle. Maybe it's for the best."

Heart pounding, she nodded, but before he could turn away, she grasped his upper arm. Hard muscles tensed beneath the fabric of his shirt and she withdrew her hand. "We shouldn't kiss again," she said firmly, her voice a little husky, but never mind. "I'm not here for fun in the sun."

"At least not with me," he said, smoothing a stray lock of hair away from her cheek.

She caught his hand and said, "That's right. Not with you."

"I'll drive you into town so you can get what you need." He gestured behind her. "Close your door and windows and lock them."

"I want to catch the breeze—"

"What you might catch is a bullet. Just close and lock."

Chapter Five

On the way through the courtyard, they passed a large, empty pool, its vibrant mosaic reminiscent of the one in the front entry. Three horses cast in bronze frolicked on an island in the middle of the pool, heads tossed, manes and tails flying, hooves all but thundering. It almost seemed like they could gallop right off their pedestal.

The pool will be filled tomorrow," Pete said.

"I can't wait to see what the fountain looks like," Elle murmured.

Pete led her to a gate which opened onto a covered deck. There they found a dozen golf carts, the sun motif painted on their hoods, each wrapped in plastic.

"They're so cute," Elle said. "What are they for?"

"Construction crews are finishing a paved road down to the beach on the other side of the headland," he said.

"A private beach, I assume."

"Like there's anything else around here. They've built cabanas in the shelter of some palms. There'll be a restaurant and a bar down there before next season. Guests will be able to drive up and down in the little carts. Or be chauffeured. He pointed at an old open-air Jeep. "Our ride isn't quite so cute. Hop in."

"I want to at least check in with the stable manager before we drive into town," Elle said as she climbed into the passenger seat.

"It's getting late," he said, glancing up at the sun. "Can't it wait until morning?"

"Alazandro hired me to help with the horses, right? Before I see the man, I'd like to have at least seen the stables. It won't take long."

The ride to the stable wasn't long and at any other time, Elle would have enjoyed the beautiful surroundings. Instead, Pete's proximity had her nerves twitching. What was she going to do about him?

She jumped out of the cart before it stopped rolling. Anxious to put a little distance between them, she strode toward the stable without looking back. Let him play catch up for a change.

The stables featured the same mission-style red-tile roofs, stucco walls and rounded, shuttered windows as the resort. The high rafters and aisle doors opened in all directions. Several equine heads looked up when she entered. The comfortable sound of men joking with one another as they mucked out a couple of the stables sounded like music to Elle, the smells and sounds of the stable all cozy and familiar.

"Do you ride horses, Pete?"

"When Alazandro rides. Last time we were here he rode every day."

"Why aren't you with him now?"

For just a second, she felt his body stiffen and then he finally said, "He's meeting with Alberto Montega…an associate."

"Did he see the doctor already?"

"He's keeping the doctor waiting. Alazandro likes to keep people waiting."

"But he doesn't like to kept waiting, right?"

"Like at the airport, no."

"So Mr. Alazandro is without a bodyguard."

"Rudy is standing outside his door, armed to the teeth."

"Why is Rudy doing this, why not you?"

He flicked an irritated set of eyes over her as he snapped, "Because Alazandro wants to make sure you arrive at his place tonight in one tasty piece."

His gaze stayed right on her face as his words filled the air between them. Elle broke the stare-off and resumed walking. "So, where's the stable manager?"

"His office is right down here." He led the way to an office piled high with papers. An empty swivel chair sat in front of a cluttered desk.

"He's probably around somewhere," Pete said.

"Looks like he has lots to keep him busy."

Pete glanced around the messy office. "He's only worked here a couple of months. The first guy got a better job offer back in the States."

"How many times have you been here with Alazandro?"

"Once before. Alazandro's been dividing his attention between Puerta Del Sol and Hawaii lately."

"Yet another resort?"

"Up in Waimea. Lots of horses up that way. Alazandro loves his horses."

"So why is he here when the resort isn't ready to open for another few weeks."

"He fired the resort manager. There are last-minute decisions to be made before a big opening." He held up a hand to still her. "Enough with the questions. I'm not

Alazandro's confidante, I'm just a lowly bodyguard paid to watch his back and keep his latest sweetheart out of trouble."

She leaned in close and whispered, "If you hate the man so much, why do you work for him?"

His expression remained the same, but something clicked behind his eyes and Elle felt a stirring of alarm.

New scenario: Pete was involved in the plot to kill Alazandro. He had the skills, he had the brains....

"The same reason you do, babe." He rubbed his thumb and two fingers together. "The man pays well. How I feel about him is irrelevant."

They both turned as a sound farther along the interior of the barn drew their attention. Elle was glad for the distraction. She wound up in front of the feed room one step ahead of Pete.

It looked a lot tidier than Peg's feed room. Several metal bins labeled with various grains and supplements occupied the right hand wall while baskets of carrots and apples hung overhead. Bags of grains, looking as though they'd just been delivered, were stacked along the left wall. A counter along the back housed a sink along with a scale, blender and a food processor for mixing. A man wearing a bright shirt bent over one open container. He seemed to be pawing through its contents.

Pete said in a louder than normal voice, "Tom? You have company."

A flushed, pudgy man lifting a big measuring cup filled with beet cubes turned abruptly. The bin lid clattered shut as some of the tiny cubes scattered on the cement floor. He pulled a blue bandana from his pocket and used it to dab at his moist face as he dumped the cubes into a pail by the sink.

"Didn't hear you come in," Tom said. He offered Elle a damp hand and added, "I was just getting a little treat ready for Rojo Grande. I don't believe we've met."

"Elle Medina. I'm new."

"Alazandro wants you to teach her the ropes," Pete said. "She speaks fluent Spanish so she can help you out."

"Jorge's been helping me," Tom said, his glance darting to a point behind Elle's shoulder.

Elle twirled in time to see a dark haired man with a drooping mustache disappear into a stall across the way and down a bit.

She turned back as Pete spoke. "Yeah, but I guess the boss doesn't totally trust Jorge. There have been grumblings that he's skimming off the top come payday."

"That's crazy—"

Pete held up a hand. "Take it up with Alazandro. He wants you to rely on Elle, not Jorge."

Tom stared at Pete for a second before finding his voice again. "Kind of busy now, though."

"Whenever it's convenient for you," Elle said. Gesturing at the pail, she added, "Rojo is the big sorrel gelding across the way, right? Maybe I could help get those cubes ready to give him later after they've—"

"No, that's okay," Tom interrupted. He picked up the pail and took a few steps, saying, "I'll just dump this in Rojo's feed tray. We've got horses coming in later so we'll be busy—"

"Aren't you going to soak them first?"

Tom turned bewildered eyes to her. "Soak what?"

"The beet cubes. They have to be soaked first. They're a great source of protein but if they aren't soaked they can choke a horse or cause colic—"

"Of course, of course," Tom interrupted, backing up to the sink. The pail clattered on the stainless steel counter as he dropped it. "I wasn't thinking." He flashed a quick, insincere smile. Elle decided that with his small, neatly centered features he resembled a boiled pink Easter egg. Only a fuzz of blondish hair protected his balding head. She guessed he was around forty.

"Come back later," Tom added. "Like about seven."

"Not tonight," Pete said, dipping his head close to hers. His voice was hardly a whisper, however, as he added, "We've got to go to town and then there's Alazandro and your midnight supper, remember?"

Elle had never realized how difficult it would be to assume such an ill-fitting identity let alone flaunt it in front of a man who made her knees weak.

She smiled sweetly. "How could I forget? Well, we better hit the road if I'm going to have enough time to get all spiffed up for Mr. Alazandro. Nice to meet you, Tom. I'll come back later." As she walked away, she glanced into the stall in which the man with the mustache had disappeared moments before.

His gaze followed her as she walked past.

THE NEAREST TOWN was five bumpy, dusty, sticky miles away. As it was over relatively flat, featureless land, there was little in the way of ambush to worry Pete.

They passed one vehicle, a big three-ton truck hauling a horse trailer back toward the resort. Elle turned in her seat to watch its retreat, her fair hair whipping around her head. He caught a glimpse of her flawless profile as she turned and almost drove off the road.

The town of Las Brisas, built on the shores of Rio Las Brisas had been bypassed by developers and tourists alike. The town was poor and this late in the summer the river was reduced to a slow, tepid stream that children and dogs played in to cool off.

Pete parked on the main street and made Elle take a fistful of pesos, arguing with her that it would be a lot easier to shop in a town this small with Mexican currency instead of dollars or credit cards.

"Tell me Mr. Alazandro's favorite color," she said as she stood in the empty street beside him.

She'd acquired a pink tone to her lightly tanned skin and if not careful, would soon have a sunburn. Making something up, he said, "Yellow. And get yourself some sunscreen."

She smiled. "Yes, sir. Thanks."

He tried to follow her but she waved him aside and as the tiny village seemed to present limited possibilities for mayhem, he didn't argue.

Besides, there was a handgun locked in the glove box and a rifle tucked under the seat. Wouldn't do to lose sight of his armory. Pete climbed back into the Jeep and angled his body to put the unrelenting sun at his back. As he waited, he tried to plan what he would tell Elle to enlist her help.

The trouble was she never reacted to a damn thing the way he thought she would. And her questions…he was the one supposed to be finding out things but he spent half his time with her fielding questions.

Well, enough was enough. His totally inappropriate feelings for her were going to get them both in big trouble if he didn't find a way to control his rampaging hormones.

And really, that's all it was, all it could be. He hadn't known her long and he'd sworn off blondes. Shari had been the last one. She'd been enough.

After Shari, in a moment of semi-drunken introspection, he'd admitted to himself that he was drawn to women in self-destruct mode. When the chance to pay back the drug dealers of the world came up, he'd grabbed it. Peter Walker became Pete Waters, the former Marine slash cop became a former disgraced cop turned documented felon and rumored hit man, someone sure to appeal to Víctor Alazandro.

A wave of frustration tightened Pete's chest. The DEA had been trying to nail this guy for a very long time, but he was slippery and deceptively smart.

Several weeks before, Pete had signed on as his bodyguard and come to Mexico with Alazandro and his entourage for the first time. Expecting instant success, he'd planted his recorders and lurked behind trees and learned absolutely nothing. Alazandro held his meetings on the rooftop three stories off the ground. He held them with very select people. He played loud music. The recorder Pete had risked life and limb to plant came back full of gobbledlygook.

Then the girl, Amber Linn, had turned up dead in Alazandro's private quarters. The police had come and gone, shaking their heads. The drugs were prescription, the kid was an American, Alazandro owned the police, the whole thing was a nonissue.

Soon after that, however, they'd left Mexico and flown to Hawaii. Pete's hopes had soared. Hawaii wasn't as remote as Puerta Del Sol. He tapped phone lines, planted recorders and wired an inside man. Everything in place, Alazandro did nothing but swim and ride horses during the day, party and womanize at night.

The informant had said it would all go down before September. They were running out of time. The fact that

Alazandro had set up a secret meeting with Alberto Montega for the first day they were back in Mexico was very interesting. It was well known Montega was high up on Ciro Ramos' payroll. Ciro Ramos had a burgeoning drug enterprise down in Mexico City. If the two were putting their heads together, Pete would bet big bucks the topic of discussion was this upcoming meeting.

It was soon. Pete could feel it in his bones.

And here he was, sitting in a Jeep, keeping an eye on the boss's would-be girlfriend.

So make the best of it. Figure out a way to use her.

He ignored the snake twisting through his gut. He'd come on to her earlier in the day, knowing the only way she might be prone to help him was if he could win over her emotions. Instead, he suspected she'd won over his.

He looked up to see her walking down the street toward him. She'd added sunglasses and a straw cowboy hat to her white shirt and jeans. Her long-legged stride ate up the gravel road. He couldn't take his eyes off of her.

She carried a fair number of bags and as she came around to the passenger door and flashed him a brilliant smile, he felt his heart kind of thump in his chest. How did she manage to look so fresh when he felt as though he'd been sprayed down with sweat and rolled in the dust?

"You done already?" he asked.

"I've got everything I need for now," she said.

"This place isn't exactly a shopping center, though it's picked up some since the resort moved in close by. What about contact lenses?"

"I brought a few extras in my purse," she said. "How do you know I wear—"

"I can see them when I look real close," he answered,

resisting the impulse to demonstrate by pulling her into his arms and ripping off the big sunglasses. "Plus, I looked at your driver's license, remember?"

She smiled as she threw the bags in the back and slid into the passenger seat. "I guess we better get back."

He pointed at the little café outside of which they'd parked. "Do you want a cold drink first? We need to talk."

She raised her eyebrows.

"Let's get a cold beer."

They claimed a shaded sidewalk table six feet away from the Jeep's rear bumper. Within moments, they each accepted an icy bottle topped with a pale wedge of lime.

They clinked bottles, then took a swallow. The cold brew felt like heaven rolling down Pete's parched throat. Elle issued a sigh of contentment, set the bottle down with a thunk, propped her elbows on the table and said, "Out with it."

"Not much for foreplay, are you?" he said with a slow smile.

"Not with you, buddy, I thought we established that. Come on, talk."

"Obviously, you're visiting Alazandro tonight."

"Obviously."

"I need you to help me with something."

She leaned forward, resting her chin on her hands. "Sounds interesting."

He traced a finger on the rustic table top and put on his humble face. "Alazandro is a private man."

"I imagine a man in his position would have to be. He's a very successful businessman. He's got a million irons in the fire. I can hardly believe he has the time of a day for a woman like me."

Was she putting him on? What was with the "woman

like her" bit? Beautiful? Sassy? Sexy as hell? He shook his head, trying to get his mind back on his plan, such as it was. He said, "Yeah. Well, anyway, he doesn't always tell me what he's up to. Makes it hard to anticipate what measures need to be taken. Not only for his sake, but as you saw in Tahoe, for the safety of those, er, close to him."

"Like me," she said.

"Well, yes. I know you're concerned about getting gunned down with him, right?"

She gulped a little as she leaned even closer. "Gunned down?"

"I don't know what else to call it. Whoever is after him is ruthless."

"Do you think so?"

He narrowed his eyes. "You know, at first I thought it might be Peg Stiles. She doesn't like the man much, does she?"

"No. But Peg isn't a killer."

"You'd be surprised, Elle, who is and isn't a killer. But it's more than that, it's the fact that you were also a target. I don't believe Peg Stiles would try to shoot you no matter how upset she was."

"I don't, either," Elle said.

"That leaves your father."

"The judge wouldn't shoot me, either," she said firmly.

"I agree."

"Leaving the unknown person who threatened Alazandro in the first place."

He shrugged. "Process of elimination."

"I can't imagine why anyone would want to kill him, though. I mean, kidnap, yes. Ransom and all that. But he's a businessman, what has he ever done to anybody?"

It took Pete a moment to neutralize his voice before saying, "Businessmen can be ruthless."

She opened her eyes wide. "You don't think he's in danger from the man who came to visit him today. What's his name, Alberto Montega?"

"No," Pete said. "They're…associates."

"You mean friends."

"Víctor Alazandro doesn't have friends, he has associates." He studied her face for a second before adding, "But that's a good example of me being shut out of Alazandro's plans. I didn't even know Montega was coming today. Who knows what other plans Alazandro has made that he isn't telling me."

She took a deep breath and sat back in her chair. Crossing one elegant leg over the other she said, "What do you want me to do?"

"Just spend as much time with him as you can. And if he says anything about people coming to visit or him going somewhere else, let me know."

"So you can be prepared."

"Exactly," he said with a smile.

She grinned as she sat up straight. "You can count on me," she said. "I'll stick as close to him as possible. I'll be his little shadow. I know I was hired to help in the stable, but maybe Mr. Alazandro needs a little extra care himself, you know? Maybe he'll like having me…around. He's so fascinating, I know I could learn a lot just by being close to him."

"Learn a lot about what?" he snapped.

"About life," she said. "I have a million questions for him."

Víctor Alazandro a teacher? Pete stifled a bark of laughter. What wasn't funny was contemplating how Alazandro would handle Elle's prying. "Don't be too obvious," he cautioned.

"I'm anxious to get back and start sleuthing. For the good of the team, I mean."

"No, not sleuthing," he said, growing increasingly alarmed by her enthusiasm. It would be so much easier if he thought of people the way Alazandro did: expendable, replaceable.

But he didn't, and the thought of Elle getting hurt because of something he set her up for made him shudder.

"Then what would you call it?" she asked.

"Listening," he said firmly. "Just listen."

"And report."

"And don't get creative."

THE DRIVE HOME was made as the sun set and the stars began to pop out in the night sky. Elle tipped her head back as the warm wind whipped through her hair.

She glanced at Pete's profile as he drove.

Nice.

The Jeep slowed down and she turned her attention back to the road. Pete downshifted as they approached a car pulled off on the shoulder.

"Someone has car trouble," she said.

"Must be someone headed for Puerta Del Sol. There's nothing else out here."

Their headlights bathed the rear bumper of an old blue sedan. Leaving the Jeep idling, Pete was in the process of stepping out when the sedan's driver's door opened without triggering a light inside the car. Elle stood up to stretch.

"Get down," Pete yelled as he launched himself back

toward the Jeep. In the next instant, the world exploded as a blasting report rent the still night air.

Elle had fallen back on her seat and she looked up to find a man advancing, dark hat pulled low over his face, rifle held out in front.

Pete was half in, half out of the truck, his cheek pressed against the leather seat, his right hand trailing down in the foot well. "Shift into gear," he yelled. Elle ground the gearshift into first. The engine gunned—Pete was pushing on the accelerator pedal with his hand. Grabbing the wheel, she yanked it toward the road, sideswiping the sedan's rear bumper as the rifleman scrambled out of the way.

Another blast from the rifle merged into the sound of metal crunching against metal as the Jeep grated against the sedan, breaking off its side-view mirror. She steered the Jeep back onto the road, Pete working the clutch as his feet all but dragged on the dirt road. Pete dragged the lower half of his body back into the Jeep. He grabbed the wheel as Elle looked behind.

"He's following," she yelled as the headlights of the other car switched on. It jounced over rocks and gullies as the sedan pulled back on the road.

"Reach in my pocket, get the key for the glove box," Pete said.

He straightened his right leg to facilitate the process causing the car to slow down for a moment. She pushed her hand into his pocket until she felt the jagged metal edge of a key. It took a moment to get it out and then another to find the lock on the glove box in the dark as her hair blew into her eyes.

"There's a gun in there," Pete said as their windshield cracked into pieces with a shattering pop.

"Did a bullet just go right between out heads?"

"Yeah. Keep down, as low as you can. Can you shoot out a tire?"

"I can try," she said, withdrawing the gun from the glove box.

"It's loaded and ready to go," Pete said.

Elle scooted down into the seat well, then wiggled back up, positioning her arm and hand to steady them. The car behind them seemed to be catching up. She cocked the gun. It was impossible to aim properly. Her gunfire was returned from the driver's side of the sedan.

"I missed."

"Just keep shooting."

"How can that guy drive and shoot?" she cried.

"Just keep shooting," Pete repeated as it seemed they hit every rut in the road.

Elle kept firing but her bullets went wild. Far ahead, the lights of the resort created a beckoning oasis of safety—if they could reach it.

"I'm out of bullets," she screamed as she popped out the empty magazine. "I need more ammo."

"There's none in the car but there's a loaded shotgun under the driver's seat," Pete yelled, looking down at her.

"Doesn't do us much good there," Elle grumbled, reaching under his seat with her right hand. The rifle was there, but it was locked into place with a mechanism she couldn't maneuver open when she couldn't even see it.

The car advanced, the sound of gunfire and pinging bullets all around. Pete, head angled as low as he could get it and still see over the wheel, shouted again.

"Hold on to the frame, stay down," he said, and Elle scooted even lower, finding the door handle and the seat frame to hold on to, the spent revolver rattling on the floor between her knees.

The car slowed down. Elle felt a scream rise up her throat, but she squelched it. Why was Pete slowing down? She raised her gaze in time to see the other car's headlights pull alongside. Pete jerked the wheel abruptly, crashing his side of the Jeep into the sedan as bullets flew over their heads. Both cars sped up and again Pete veered sharply left. By the third or fourth time he'd done it, they'd pushed the other vehicle toward the far shoulder of the road. Pete yanked the steering wheel one last time.

Elle looked up in time to see the sedan bounce off the road. For a second, it seemed it might roll, but the driver managed to pull it out of the ditch. As the Jeep sped toward Puerta Del Sol, the sedan stopped, its headlights illuminating a fan shaped wedge of scrappy vegetation.

Elle sat back in her seat. She expected Pete to unlock the rifle and return to the sedan to find out who was behind the shooting, but he kept going, accelerating even faster.

"What are you doing?" she yelled.

He shifted into high gear. "I'm getting you the hell out of here," he said.

"Go back!"

"No way."

"But—"

"If anything happens to you, Alazandro will cut my throat," he said, turning to face her, his expression grim. "I'll come back. Alone."

Though the last thing in the world she wanted was for him to return alone to face the men in the car, further protest died on her lips.

Within minutes, they passed the guards at the gate,

Pete slowing long enough to tell them not to allow anyone else in. He pulled up in front of the arched doorway. They both jumped out of the Jeep. As Elle came around to his side, Pete grabbed her bags from the back as she captured her new hat. It was amazing it hadn't flown out of the back seat during the chase.

"I'll walk you to your room," he said.

She shrugged him off and grabbed her shopping bags from his hands. "Go. I'll be fine."

"Stay in your room," he said. He reached under the front seat and in one quick motion, unclamped the rifle from under the driver's seat, laying it in the passenger's seat beside him.

He looked back at her, his eyes full of some emotion she couldn't begin to name. She blinked her eyes rapidly as she stared at him. Tall, strong, in warrior mode.

"Get someone to go with you," she urged. "Don't go alone. They could be waiting, it could be a trap—"

"I'm counting on it," he said, and with a squeal of tires, was gone.

Chapter Six

Elle unlocked her door with steady fingers, flicked on every light from the panel beside the door and looked around before entering. But the suite was huge, providing many places for someone to hide. She looked in every corner, succumbing to the shakes only when she knew she was absolutely alone.

She hated being sequestered. She hated not seeing who had done such an outrageous thing and finding out why. And most of all she hated thinking what might be happening to Pete at that very moment.

She ran an impatient hand through her hair and winced as her fingers came away gritty. *Can't play the femme fatale with dirty hair.* She looked down at her clothes for the first time. The formerly white blouse was now smudged with dirt and grease. She had to shower and get ready for Alazandro. She had to concentrate.

A half hour later, she sat on the edge of the bed, clean, dressed and close to shaking herself right out of her new sandals. Where was Pete? Why hadn't he come back? It was almost time to see Alazandro, but she realized that even if she knew the way to his room, she couldn't go without first knowing Pete was all right.

Pete had given her a gift that evening. He'd asked her to listen to Alazandro which was just what she wanted. Without Pete scowling at her all the time, she could concentrate on finding out the truth.

She heard a sound outside her door. In a flash she threw it open while in the back of her head a long ago voice warned never to open the door to strangers.

PETE LEANED AGAINST THE DOORJAMB, shotgun in one hand. The door opened before he could even knock and Elle stood there, eyes wide.

"You okay?" he said.

She started to throw herself at him and he held out a hand to stop her. "I'm filthy," he said, looking her new dress up and down.

Somewhere in that tiny village she'd found herself a pale yellow sundress with tiny straps and a plunging neckline. She wore no jewelry. Hell, she needed no jewelry. She looked stunning, perfect, like a fragile flower, plucked from the vine and set before his eyes.

"I was worried sick about you," she said, gaze narrowing in what he was beginning to understand was her annoyed look.

"Nothing to be worried about," he said lightly. "The sedan was long gone by the time I got back."

"So we don't know who was chasing us."

"There are a million old blue sedans in Mexico. It was too dark to get much more than a glimpse of the man who got out of the car."

"Tall," she said.

"Made taller by the rifle at his side," Pete said with a smile.

"Which one of us do you think he was after?"

Pete stared at her as he tried to decide what to say. He wanted her to be cautious, but he didn't want to scare her to death, either. He settled on the truth. "Me. If someone is after Alazandro then it makes sense they would try to take out his bodyguards. I'll alert the others." He looked at her closely and added, "Unless there's something you're not telling me. Someone want you dead, Elle? A jilted lover maybe? An irate creditor? Is your murky past finally catching up with you?"

"I don't have a murky past," she said. "How did you know to jump out of the way before the first shot was fired?"

"The light didn't go when the door opened."

"That's it?"

"I had precious cargo," he said without thinking.

They looked at each other without blinking for a moment. Pete didn't know what thoughts occupied her—he only knew his were all across the board. Relief she was okay, lust because she looked so damn hot, and regret she was not dolled up to impress him, that she didn't give a damn what he thought.

He wanted to nudge those tiny straps right off her shoulders and watch the dress slide past her breasts, down her hips, along her legs and pool at her feet. He wanted to see her naked, and he wanted her to want him with that deep wrenching ache that had settled in his groin the moment he laid eyes on her. He said, "Nice dress."

She turned in a little circle, setting the skirt swirling around her legs. "Do you think Mr. Alazandro will like it?" As she moved, a delicate scent wafted over him. Soap or shampoo or some subtle perfume, something as light as the brush of a lover's first kiss.

He grunted.

She said, "I guess it's time to go. I don't want to keep Mr. Alazandro waiting."

"I was due to relieve Rudy Martinez an hour ago," he said, turning away from her. Holding the shotgun in his right hand, he waited for her to lock her door. "Stay close," he growled as they moved away from her suite.

As they entered the courtyard, Pete kept his gaze peeled for a sign of their assailants. He could hear the soft click of Elle's heeled sandals on the rock path beside him, the swish of her dress as she moved. His gaze traveled the well-lit paths leading to Alazandro's private apartment, taking in every bush and shadow, but knowing full well that he could no more see every cranny than fly to the moon.

It gave him some comfort that the perimeter of the resort was guarded by armed sentries at night when Alazandro was in residence. However, over the years it had been repeatedly ground into his brain that any chain is only as strong as its weakest link. One well-placed bribe and all bets were off. He was still a little spooked by the audacity of the earlier assault.

And it irked the hell out of him not to move heaven and earth to find out what it had been about.

But what could he do? Call the police? Insist the resort be locked down? All of the above would spook Alazandro and a spooked Alazandro would not hold meetings. A spooked Alazandro would get back on his plane and fly away.

He couldn't chance that, not now when they were so close. But he would have to make sure Elle was protected.

The pool area occupied the center of the courtyard. Motioning with the barrel of the shotgun, Pete kept his voice low as he said, "We'll skirt the pool. Alazandro's quarters are behind that large mosaic at the far end."

With his last word, every light on the premises went out, casting the place into pitch black. Pete immediately raised the shotgun, but he could hear nothing except some far off voices.

"Take my hand," he said, reaching for Elle. She slipped her hand into his and he picked up the pace, using the lighter rock of the path to guide their steps.

"What happened to the electricity?" she said, taking two steps to his one.

"Power outage. They aren't all that unusual. The contractors are still ironing out the bugs."

The pool and its surrounding foliage were darker than anything else, and he steered her clear of it. Pete expected to hear voices grow louder as he headed toward the mosaic wall, but if anything the silence grew even more pronounced.

The hum of the generator sounded and some of the lights flickered on as they entered the short passage that led from behind the mosaic to Alazandro's apartment.

The relief was short lived.

"I thought you said someone was standing guard outside Mr. Alazandro's door," Elle said.

"I did." Ushering Elle in front of him, Pete hurried to the large bulletproof glass doors and knocked hard. The curtain slid open and Alazandro stood there, arm in a sling, rakish white bandage on his forehead, wearing what looked like white pajamas covered with a blood-red robe.

Alazandro slid open the lock. "Where in the hell is Rudy?" he demanded.

"I don't know. When's the last time you saw him?"

"A half hour or so before the lights went out. I must have dozed off. The lights were off when I awoke. Maybe Rudy went to see what was wrong."

There were two ways to skirt the mosaic. Pete said, "He must have gone the other way, then, because we didn't pass him. I don't see how we could have missed him. Damn, I told him to stick to this door like glue."

"Fire him."

Pete looked at Alazandro. "Let's find him first. Everything okay in there?" he added, glancing over Alazandro's head.

"Except for the blasted power outage, everything is fine." His attention darted to Elle. "Hello," he said, his eyes devouring her. Pete saw a light flush steal up Elle's neck as she joined Alazandro inside.

"Lock the door again," Pete blustered to hide a growing sense of irritation he blamed on Rudy's absence. "Stay inside until I get back."

Alazandro snaked an arm around Elle's waist. "Pete's paid to overreact, *muñeca*. While he finds Rudy, we'll drink champagne and get to know one another better." His fingers ran down Elle's bare arm. Pete had to turn away before he said something out of character.

"The kitchen is sending over lobster salad for supper," Alazandro added, his voice reaching full schmooze. "How does that sound?"

Before Elle could answer, Pete closed the door and waited for Alazandro to lock it.

The most likely scenario was that Rudy had gone to find someone to start the generator even though he shouldn't have. But even if that was true, the generator had started within minutes so why wasn't Rudy back? That was the trouble with almost any organization—

people did the unexpected. Pete's mind was on this as he rounded the mosaic, fully expecting to find a sheepish Rudy returning to his post.

A scream came from the pool area. Pete ran toward it, breaking through the lush landscape.

A woman holding a covered tray stood beside the pool. When she heard Pete's footsteps on the rock deck, she turned, eyes growing wide at the sight of him. Throwing up her hands, she dropped the tray. Lettuce and crystal rained down on her feet, spilling over the lip of the pool. She stared openmouthed at Pete, obviously scared speechless.

He recognized her from the kitchen staff. When he finally realized he'd unconsciously leveled the shotgun at her chest, he quickly lowered the muzzle. *"¿Tu nombre es Rosa, sí?"*

Rosa, apparently reassured by Pete knowing her name, turned her attention back to the pool and pointed.

Taking several steps, Pete joined her, avoiding the lobster salad and broken china.

The sparse lighting created heavy shadows in the deep end of the pool, but a darker shape was obviously human, arms and legs splayed like a squished bug on a windshield.

Rosa bit her knuckle as she turned to Pete, her face two shades more pale than it had been a moment before. After Pete helped her to a chair, he laid the shotgun aside, jumped down into the four-foot end of the empty pool and walked toward the deep end, skirting the pedestal which supported the bronze horses.

The closer he got, the more certain he became there was no life left in the person he approached. Kneeling beside the man, he rolled the body part way over. Even in the lousy light, even though his features had been smashed and were covered with blood, Pete could make out Rudy Martinez's gold front tooth. He felt Rudy's throat for a pulse. He didn't expect to find one and he didn't.

He let the body roll back, pulled the wallet out of Rudy's pocket. Rudy Martinez had carried a picture in his wallet of his two little kids.

Pete looked up to see Rosa standing by the side of the pool again, hugging herself as tears rolled down her cheeks. He knew the police should be called. Having been a cop for eight years himself, he knew this apparently unattended death needed to be investigated.

Was it supposed to look as though Rudy had rushed off to help with the generator and accidentally cast himself into the deep end of an empty swimming pool?

His body was positioned at the end of the pool, head facing toward the center like he'd taken a header. A twelve-foot drop would account for the condition of his face and the broken neck that probably killed him. But if Rudy had been conscious, wouldn't he have desperately tried to stop the fall? Would he have landed on his face with his arms akimbo?

And wouldn't Pete and Elle have heard Rudy running even if he had come from around the far corner and not been on a collision course with them? But he'd last been seen thirty minutes before the lights went out. A lot can happen in thirty minutes.

Rosa whispered, "¿Policía?"

Facts were facts. Alazandro owned the local police. There would be no legitimate autopsy, Rudy's body would be shipped back to his family. It was all reminiscent of Amber Linn's death a few months before.

"No," Pete called up to Rosa as he retraced his steps to the shallow end of the pool and hoisted himself back to the deck. He'd tell Alazandro about Rudy before calling in the local cops. He'd remain undercover, a paid bodyguard whose sole purpose was to protect Alazandro's life and his business interests. There was more at stake here than discovering the truth about one man's death.

Apologies to Rudy Martinez, his widow and his father-less children, that was just the way it was.

A CROWD GATHERED in the courtyard as the police took away Rudy's body. Elie's gaze met with that of the pilot and the copilot. Both men looked as rattled as she felt and returned her nod of acknowledgment with a disbelieving shake of their heads before disappearing back inside the resort.

She looked around for Pete and found him standing at the deep end of the pool, staring down. He looked up and his expression went from angry to introspective. For some reason she was reminded of an actor assuming a role.

What did she know about him? For instance, was he married? He sure didn't kiss like a married man….

They began walking toward each other. When she got close enough, he pulled her against his side in a broth-erly embrace. It didn't feel brotherly, though, and this time it wasn't his fault, it was hers.

Still, his protective arm helped soothe the shock of un-expected death. She closed her eyes and for a second the headache she'd come by via two hastily consumed glasses of champagne seemed to recede. She was infinitely grateful she didn't have to make more conversation with Víctor Alazandro.

Alazandro himself was noticeably absent from the

scene. After an hour or so, he'd washed his hands of this situation and gone to bed. She'd heard Pete assign two guards to stay with him.

"So, what did you and Alazandro talk about before all this happened?" Pete asked her.

"Talk about? Oh, you mean did he mention any plans you need to know about? No, mostly he grumbled because the doctor has forbidden him to ride a horse for a few more days. Listen, Pete, are you married?"

He arched away from her, searching her face. He finally said, "Do you think I'd kiss you like that if I was married?"

"Well, are you?"

"No."

"Why did you pause before answering?"

"I was trying to figure out why you wanted to know."

"I'm the nosy one, remember? So, have you ever been married?"

"Yes, once. Way back when. Right after high school, as a matter of fact. She had blond hair."

Elle smiled. "What happened to her?"

"I don't know. We were only married for a few weeks before I shipped out in the Marines. She divorced me while I was gone. Fell hopelessly in love with the guy who groomed her cocker spaniel."

"You're kidding."

"Nope. Last I heard she had moved to Minnesota with the groomer. We don't stay in touch." He paused for a second before adding, "You should go to bed."

"What if this wasn't an accident?"

"The police say—"

"But the police don't know someone attacked us earlier tonight. Or did you tell them?"

"No, I didn't tell them. Did you?"

"No. Aren't you the least bit suspicious?"

"The only reason to take out a bodyguard is to get to the body it's guarding. If someone tried to get me earlier tonight and then Rudy, it didn't work because Alazandro is sleeping like a baby. Maybe it really was an accident. We'll probably never know."

"You have to tell the police about earlier tonight—"

"The police work for Alazandro," he said, leaning close to whisper.

She drew back and stared at him. "But then they should try twice as hard to see if Rudy's death was really an accident. They'll want to protect Mr. Alazandro."

"It doesn't work that way," Pete said softly.

"I don't understand."

"Alazandro won't want controversial press. He takes care of problems internally. The fact is it doesn't matter if Rudy's death was an accident or not as far as the police are concerned. This place is opening soon. It's given umpteen jobs to locals and will bring in lots more money once it's going. No one here wants any bad publicity."

"I can't believe no one cares."

"Elle, do yourself a favor and go home. You can catch a ride north with the pilot tomorrow—"

"No," she said.

"It's dangerous—"

"Not for me! You said it yourself, it's Alazandro's bodyguards who are in danger. If I stay away from you, I ought to be safe."

"You don't know that for sure," he insisted.

"I'm not an idiot."

"Then don't act like one. Go home. Don't let greed get you killed."

"*You're* calling *me* greedy?" she said, rubbing her fingers and thumb together like he had earlier.

"Elle—"

"Good night," she said firmly. She walked away. Within a few steps, it was obvious he was hot on her heels. She turned and sighed, "Now what?"

"Nothing. Pretend I'm not here."

"No problem," she said and continued on her way. The last thing she saw when she closed and locked her door was Pete standing a few feet away, shotgun tipped up against his shoulder.

He flipped her a smart salute.

Chapter Seven

Elle rose early the next morning. Her eyes felt like sandpaper.

She'd gone to bed at 3:00 a.m. and slept restlessly, plagued by the old dream again. No doubt the violence of the day before had stimulated the nightmare for the second night in a row. She left her suite after a quick change into her dusty jeans and a new pink T-shirt.

The sprinklers were on in the courtyard, taking advantage of the early morning cool. Mist settled on her skin and she took a couple of deep, fragrant breaths. Two workmen were in the process of filling the swimming pool.

Would Rudy have survived his fall into the pool had it been full last night? Or had he been dead before he ever left the rim?

Elle could see how Pete would be duty bound to follow Alazandro's orders to keep things quiet, but it all seemed so odd. The silence worked to her advantage, however, as she had a purpose of her own and fulfilling that purpose took top priority.

Today she had to get Alazandro to talk about Seattle again. The sooner everything was wrapped up, the better.

Last night had left no doubt in her mind what Alazandro's intentions concerning her were.

And then there was Pete and that growing attraction between them that could not end well. He'd signed on to protect the man she'd signed on to kill—if she had to.

Lost in thought, Elle walked behind the mosaic and ran smack into a very large man carrying an even larger weapon. He held up a hand and Elle stopped abruptly.

In Spanish, she asked to see Alazandro.

The man stared at her.

She explained she was a friend, this time in English.

He was a good foot taller than Elle, a hundred pounds heavier with a bald head roughly the size and shape of a bowling ball. She tried a few words of broken Japanese even though she was sure he was Chinese but she knew no Chinese. It didn't matter. No matter what she said or in what language she said it, he regarded her without blinking. She gave up after a few minutes of one-sided conversation.

It was obvious Alazandro took the threats on his life seriously. She had to get close to him before he became so nervous he wouldn't trust her. Frustrated, she made her way to the barn. If a few hours spent in the company of beautiful horses couldn't pick her up, nothing could.

The trailer carrying horses they'd passed the night before sat parked in front one of the outbuildings in back of the barn. Several men were off-loading fifty pound bags of grain and feed from a big truck pulled up beside the trailer. She followed one man wheeling three huge bags into the barn. As he continued down the center aisle, she paused to talk to a couple of men filling the water buckets in each stall, running her hand down the white blaze of a docile mare with huge brown eyes.

The barn was again a haven of familiar smells and sounds. Talking and joking with the men made her more comfortable than she had been in twenty-four hours. Of course, she wasn't at Puerta Del Sol to be comfortable, but being part of the world in the barn, exchanging jokes and banter with nice people doing work they enjoyed felt a hundred times more restful than the few hours sleep she'd managed since leaving Tahoe.

She passed Jorge loitering in the stable near Tom Meacham's office. He glowered at her before sauntering through the outside door into the paddock beyond.

Tom Meacham was going over invoices. "Morning," she called from his doorway.

He fumbled a few papers and turned in his swivel chair. He didn't seem to remember who she was.

"Elle Medina, we met yesterday," she coaxed.

"Of course." Papers showered around his feet as he stood.

"I came to ask what you need me to do," she said, helping him pick up the papers.

"Have a seat," he offered, pointing a handful of papers toward a semi-empty chair to his right.

Elle handed him what she'd collected, then moved a few catalogues and sat down, placing the catalogues back on her lap. She said, "I didn't get a chance to look around much yesterday evening—"

"Wasn't that terrible about Rudy Martinez?"

"Horrible," Elle said. They sat in silence for a moment. Elle broke it by saying, "What would you like me to do, Mr. Meacham? I can muck out stables or exercise horses." Thinking about the beet cubes from the day before, she added, "Or maybe I could take over feeding—"

"There are plenty of stable hands for things like that. They wouldn't appreciate you taking their jobs."

"Oh. Well, Pete Waters said something about the stable hands being unhappy about someone skimming wages. I could talk to the men or help with the books—"

She stopped as Tom waved a finger in a small circle. "Tempest in a teapot. Anyway, payday is a few days away."

Elle fought a rising wave of irritation. One thing she knew about stables was that there were never enough willing hands to do all the work. "I could groom, perhaps, or train—"

He shook his head.

"Okay. Well, I assume some of the horses that arrived last night might need extra care—"

"There were two grooms traveling with them. They'll be off again in a few hours."

"Then I could help get them ready for transport—"

"No need."

She sighed deeply. Why was he stonewalling her? "Then I'll help unload the supply truck. Surely they'll appreciate an extra set of helping hands."

Tom leaned his bulk forward in his chair. "Don't count on it."

"I'm not going to just go away," Elle said with conviction. "Like it or not, Mr. Alazandro hired me to help you and that's what I'm going to do."

He chewed on the end of his pencil for a moment before shifting his weight in the chair. "I guess there's one thing. The boss wants a fancy ride for the rich guys."

She said, "Pardon?"

"You know, we have trails here, some really nice ones. But the boss wants something special."

Elle sat up a little. "The guys were talking while they were filling the water buckets. They mentioned something about a beach a few miles south of here—"

Tom held up a hand. "That's too far away. I like the sound of a place called Copper Mesa. It's—" he paused, swiveling his chair to find the right direction "—that way. East of here."

"Inland? You don't think a ride along the ocean might be prettier and cooler?"

He stared right into her eyes and said, "No, I don't. Too much trouble."

"But—"

"I'm the boss," he said, a flicker of steel in his mild eyes that surprised Elle.

"Yes. I know."

"Someone needs to see how the trail up to Copper Mesa looks, see how hard it would be to cater a lunch up there. I was going to use a helicopter, but it would be better to check it out on a horse. You could take someone with you to see what needs to be done to improve it."

Elle sighed. It was still early morning, but it was already hot. He was trying to get rid of her, she'd bet a bundle on that. On the other hand, if she couldn't question Alazandro, the next best thing was riding. "Sure," she said. "Of course."

The corners of Tom's small mouth twitched as he said, "Take Carlos with you. He doesn't hardly say boo so you'll have a quiet ride. I think he's out in the pasture."

Elle got up from the chair, replaced the catalogues and left to find Carlos, her goal to get underway before Pete found a reason to stop her.

She hadn't yet wandered around in the barn and it took her a second or two to get her bearings. She walked into the stall in which Jorge had lurked the day before. Like all the others, this one was covered with rubber matting, top-notch quality from the look of it, clean straw scattered over top.

Elle exited the stall into a paddock that led to the pasture. She could see a man near one of the fences, bathing the big sorrel.

At that moment, she felt a presence behind her and turned to find Jorge. She hadn't heard his approach.

In Spanish, he told her he'd overhead her talking to Tom Meacham. Elle wondered if there was anything that happened in that barn that Jorge didn't overhear.

He was taller than she'd realized, with broad shoulders and powerful looking arms. He wore black jeans and a black shirt. With his drooping mustache and licorice-colored eyes, he looked like someone sent out of central casting to fill the role of villain.

"Excuse me, I'm just going to talk to Carlos," she said, turning to escape Jorge's dark gaze.

He caught her arm, releasing it at once when she paused. *"No. Te llevaré al Copper Mesa,"* he said.

Elle wasn't sure how to respond. He hadn't asked her if he could take her to Copper Mesa, he'd told her. She was on the verge of telling him to get lost when he added that he was the only one who knew the exact location of the mesa's only manageable trail. Without waiting for her to respond, he walked back through the stall into the barn. Elle followed a little more meekly than suited her.

But when she thought about it, Tom had sneered when he'd said Carlos didn't talk a lot. The more she knew about Alazandro, his stable, his horses and his business, the better. Jorge might be just the man.

Also, she wouldn't put it past Tom Meacham to have assigned her a guide who didn't know the way.

PETE SAT across from Alazandro, watching the man carve his sunny-side up eggs using a fork balanced precariously in his left hand. Though he'd lost the head bandage, his right arm was still in a sling.

Alazandro pierced the last limp piece of yolk-stained egg white, carefully slid it onto a toast point, put down his fork and popped the morsel into his mouth. He wiped his lips with the corner of his napkin and took a satisfied breath.

Why didn't men like Víctor Alazandro get coronary disease like everyone else? Sure would save the government a lot of money.

"So what happened to Rudy Martinez last night?" Alazandro said.

"What was the official police decision?" Pete hedged.

"One-hundred percent accident."

Pete shrugged. "I can't think why anyone would want to kill the man."

"The most likely reason would be to get to me," Alazandro said around a swallow of mango juice. "If Rudy was gone before the lights went off, why didn't they come attack me?"

Pete kept his face impassive, but Alazandro had asked a good question.

Alazandro glanced at his watch. "Keep your ears and eyes open." He pushed himself away from the table and stood.

"How about this afternoon?" Pete said. "Are you expecting Señor Montega again?"

Alazandro looked up from the newspaper he'd focused on. "Perhaps. Why do you ask?"

"It's hard to provide adequate protection when I don't know who's coming and going."

"You check everyone who comes in here for weapons?"

"Yeah," Pete said.

Alazandro shrugged his one good shoulder.

Pete said, "I was thinking about Elle Medina."

This caught Alazandro's full attention. "What do you mean?"

"She's been very anxious to spend more time with you."

Alazandro's leer just begged to be knocked off his face. "I think she has kind of a schoolgirl crush on me," he said. "It's flattering. Don't worry, she'll get what she wants and I'll get what I want."

Pete swallowed hard and made something up. "Well, since last night was such a bust, she wants to know if she can see you this afternoon."

Alazandro stood slack faced for a second, then scratched his slightly crooked nose with his left forefinger. "She might amuse Montega," he said at last.

Pete mentally counted to ten. His feet felt funny, like they were about an inch off the floor. He relaxed his clenched fist as he said, "What do you mean?"

"There's something about a beautiful woman's presence that softens a man, Pete. Okay, tell the kitchen to send lunch up to the rooftop two hours after Montega arrives. And tell Elle to join us at that time. You, too."

Pete, who had started walking to the door, stopped and turned. He couldn't believe his ears. He was going to be present during Montega's visit? He said, "I'll come on up with Mr. Montega, sir. After last night, I don't want to leave you without a bodyguard in attendance."

"You called my stateside security outfit last night, didn't you? I told you who to ask for. Is he here yet?"

"Shen Kuai flew in a couple of hours ago. He's guarding your door right now. I'll be on the roof with you and leave him down by the door—"

"When Montega comes send up Shen Kuai. He doesn't speak a word of English or Spanish."

"You don't trust your own men?" Pete said. "You don't trust me?"

Alazandro's smile didn't move past his lips. "You can't divulge what you don't know."

Pete glowered. He figured even a bodyguard wouldn't appreciate that kind of comment.

"And then when Elle comes up for lunch, get rid of Shen Kuai. I want her relaxed. She knows you. He's a little, well, off-putting for a lady."

"Sure," Pete said, not even trying to hide the disgust in his voice. "I'm just a big, dumb puppy dog."

Alazandro barked out a laugh.

A soft knock on the glass drew their attention. Pete opened the door to find Shen Kuai standing next to a man Pete vaguely recognized from the stable.

Alazandro snapped, *"Ven para aca,"* to the man who followed orders by ducking quickly inside. Looking at Pete, Alazandro added, "You can go now."

Pete let himself out. So that was how Alazandro knew about pay skimming. It figured he'd have spies in the stable.

JORGE DID TURN OUT TO BE a talkative companion at first. He asked Elle a dozen questions about her life. Where she lived, what was it like, why she was in Mexico. When she tried the same gambit on him, however, he reined his horse in behind hers and clammed up.

Elle was left to ponder the reason Tom thought this hot, boring ride would entice high-rolling patrons. The only challenging part was the trail up the south side of the mesa, and that was only because the rocks were loose. Once atop, the panoramic view of the plateau below and the ocean beyond was lovely, if repetitive. There wasn't an ounce of shade. And what about the horses? Copper Mesa was huge, but there was no water. She already felt bad for her mount and for Jorge's.

When she inadvertently moved too close to a vertical drop, Jorge caught her arm and pulled her back. Rocks tumbled down the steep side of the mesa.

"Cuidadosa, señorita," he said, his black eyes boring into hers.

Careful, indeed. Elle looked back at the sheer drop. The rocks she'd displaced left a trail of dust as they skittered downward.

Would a fall from the face of the mesa kill a person?

She tried to gauge the distance.

It might. In fact, it probably would. She became very still. It seemed the dry, hot air collapsed inside her lungs as her mind raced.

Was this the way to avenge her family?

Could she do it?

Could she lure Alazandro to this mesa, to this ledge?

Could she use her own hands to push him to his death?

If he confessed, could she do it? Did she have the guts? The will?

She closed her eyes as twenty years of nightmare images filled her head.

And knew the answer.

PETE THREW HIS HAT onto the ground as he said, "She did what?"

Tom Meacham folded his hands over his belly as he repeated himself. "She went riding out to Copper Mesa with Jorge. I told her to take Carlos, but she rode off with Jorge. Carlos said she never asked him. At least, I think that's what he said. I can't understand much—"

Pete held up a hand to stop Tom's prattling. He shook his head as he ran a hand through his short hair.

He'd seen her walking down to the barn that morning as he went to Alazandro's apartment and he'd smiled to himself. He'd thought the barn an excellent place for her. She'd be in her element, she'd be out of trouble and with all the locals around, she'd be safe. He would know where to find her when he wanted her. He'd left her alone figuring he'd come get her at the last moment.

Now she was off alone with Jorge.

Sometimes he missed being a regular cop living in his quite little hometown of Santa Barbara, California. Jogging on the beach. Eating seafood down at the pier. Chasing regular crooks and ne'er-do-wells. Flirting with girls who had the decency to flirt back.

"Truth is, I just wanted to get rid of her. She's kind of, well…stubborn. Rambled on about a beach. Who cares?"

Pete leaned over and picked his hat up off the floor. Brushing away a few wayward pieces of straw, he said, "Yeah. She is stubborn. Part of her charm."

As he left the barn, he looked up the road leading to the east and swore under his breath. He wanted to be up on the roof with Alazandro and Montega but he wasn't welcome without Elle. She was his golden ticket and she was off riding around the countryside with brooding Jorge of all people.

At least he hoped that was all that was happening. The thought of Elle all alone with that man made something in Pete's jaw clench. Maybe he should saddle up and ride out toward Copper Mesa. He was on his way back to the barn when one last glance over his shoulder revealed an earthbound dust cloud approaching. Squinting, he could make out two horses and their riders.

About time.

He waited impatiently until they rode up next to him. Elle looked more vibrant than the overhead sun. She took off her hat and wiped her brow as she looked down at him.

"Alazandro wants you as of about right now," he barked.

"I'll be there as soon as I cool down my horse and—"

"Let someone else do that," he said, taking hold of bridle noseband. He was angry with her for disappearing with Jorge and angry at himself for worrying about her. Elle slipped from the saddle, landing with a thump. "I take care of my own—"

"We don't have time for this," Pete interrupted. He glanced up at Jorge. *"Cuidado de la toma de su caballo. Por favor."*

Jorge dismounted and took the reins of both horses, his gaze as insolent as ever. Pete grabbed Elle's elbow and more or less pushed her toward the resort.

She dug in her heels and turned to face him. "Of all the high-handed—"

"For someone so determined to stick around, you seem to have forgotten why you're here," he said.

She grew very still. "Why I'm here?"

"Alazandro expects the people who work for him to jump when he says jump. Right now he wants a beautiful woman—you—to entertain one of his friends and you look like hell."

Eyes blazing, she growled, "Why is it that half of the time we're together I want to slap you?"

"And the other half of the time you want to jump my bones. I don't know. Why is that?"

"Oh, forget it," she snapped, and took off toward the resort at a pretty good clip. He followed at a more leisurely pace, relieved when she neglected to go to her own apartment to freshen up. Alazandro would be appalled by her dusty clothes and wild hair. He wouldn't see the fire, the sparks, the way that denim hugged her bottom—

Nope. Old Alazandro was predictable. He'd expect Elle to be a hottie like she'd been the night before. Maybe he'd send her away. Then she'd be safe….

It took Pete almost three steps to remember that if Elle got sent away, so did he.

ALAZANDRO'S APARTMENT was not only lavish, it was huge and she'd seen very little of it the night before. Elle paused for a second, expecting Alazandro to materialize out of the woodwork.

"That way," Pete said from behind her. As she climbed, the sound of music grew louder.

The stairs opened into a large bedroom done in white and maize. The room was empty but glass doors stood ajar. She walked through them to find herself on a blinding white stucco deck complete with a small but sparkling swimming pool and a couple of lounge chairs. Another set of stairs jogged off at a crazy angle, as though leading straight to heaven. A Mexican love song came from the top of the stairs. Loud.

The big Asian man Elle had run into earlier that day

stood at the foot of the stairs. With one look at Pete, he disappeared inside the apartment.

Elle took off her hat and ran a hand through her wind-blown hair. She took the steps with the same energy that had driven her since she'd turned her back on Pete.

The stairs emptied onto a large triangular rooftop patio with a panoramic view of blue ocean stretching far to the horizon. Alazandro's apartment was at the tip of the headland. To the right, Elle could see the private beach and the road construction underway to create access. To the north, the coast appeared forbidding and mountainous.

Scattered pots of flowers set off the white wicker and fluttering umbrellas. Sometime within the past few moments, a breeze had come up, rustling the fronds of the potted palms. Not that she could hear them. A CD player sitting atop a low table all but obliterated other sound.

Alazandro, dressed in natural linen slacks and a saffron shirt with a matching sling, flicked off the CD player as Elle approached. The sudden quiet was almost deafening.

The other man was somewhat older and taller than Alazandro and outweighed him by about thirty pounds. Dressed more formally in sharply pleated tan slacks and a blue shirt, he wore a gold chain around his neck, one diamond earring and a chunky bracelet. A black ponytail trailed down his back.

"Elle Medina, this is my associate, Alberto Montega." Alazandro's glance traveled Elle in that proprietary way he had that made her skin crawl before adding as an aside to Montega, "Elle is my newest employee."

Elle exchanged pleasantries while Pete moved to an umbrella-covered bar and found himself a cold can of juice. She watched him out of the corner of her eye as he opened it and took a swallow. He was dressed in jeans and a denim shirt, sleeves rolled up. He'd taken off his hat and flipped it onto a chair. He regarded her with eyes made all the more blue by the backdrop of sky. Next to the other men, he appeared rangy, weathered, out of sorts and dusty.

And hot. Sexy. Virile. Elle would be willing to bet any red-blooded woman put face to face with these three men would peel off her clothes for Pete.

Why did her mind do this to her? What did she care what Pete looked like? He was acting like a jerk.

She fanned her warm face with her hat as she moved to the waist-high wall. She hadn't noticed before, but this point of the patio jutted away from everything else like the prow of a ship, so that it seemed to float over the steep drop to the rocky shore beneath.

For one long moment, she was reminded of the plan she'd hatched on the mesa.

This rooftop was handier.

"Elle?"

Turning, she plastered a smile on her face. "I'm sorry I'm late and dressed like this, Mr. Alazandro. I didn't want to keep you waiting any longer than I already had. I rode out to Copper Mesa this morning—"

"Go wash up," Alazandro said, his eyes level with hers. Where Jorge's gaze had been intimidating, Alazandro's was arrogant. "Use my shower," he added. "There are feminine necessities in the right-hand closet. Make yourself attractive and do it quickly. A very late lunch will be served in fifteen minutes and I expect you to be here."

A million retorts formed in her head and slipped away as she bit her bottom lip to keep from exploding. For all intents and purposes, she was Alazandro's showpiece— a designation that fit her goals perfectly.

"I'll be back in a moment," she said with a self-effacing smile and, leaning forward, kissed his cheek. He pulled her against him before she could move away and planted a lusty kiss on her lips. Elle made herself return the kiss as Pete's gaze burned holes in the back of her head.

Damn him.

Chapter Eight

Pete, with an impassive expression on his face, fixed rounds of drinks for everyone but himself. He was sticking to bottled water in case a horde of assassins stormed the patio. Besides, maybe someone would say something that would give him an idea of what Alazandro and Alberto were up to with these daily meetings.

Elle had returned within the allotted time, freshly scrubbed, wearing a wraparound yellow dress that molded every curve. Her hair dried in the breeze as he watched. She looked like a sunflower.

He had an ache in his temples that almost drowned out conversation. By the time the three finished their grilled fish lunch, Elle giggling and flirting up a storm with both men, he was ready to swallow a handful of aspirin. Instead he sat off to the side, trying to be invisible, trying not to look as frustrated as he felt.

Elle kept talking about Alazandro's past in Seattle. He made a mental note to ask her to move the conversation forward a little, on to something more pertinent. He knew what she was doing. She'd originally come from Seattle herself and she was trying to create a bond between them. She had no way of knowing that Alazandro didn't bond with people. Not even when he kissed them the way he'd kissed Elle. And not even when they kissed him back.

He zeroed in on the conversation as Alazandro waved an impatient hand. "Enough about Seattle," he said. Apparently explaining himself to Montega, he added, "I was just a kid trying to break into the world." He paused to laugh and added, "Let's just say there was one cop dead, another cop out to get me. Who can build a future on that? As soon as their so called proof disappeared, I took off."

"It's just so unfair," Elle said, her voice so choked with emotion she could barely speak.

Alazandro turned his attention back to her. "It all happened a lifetime ago and didn't hurt my prospects. Enhanced them as a matter of fact. Now, tell me about Copper Mesa. What were you doing out there?"

Elle took a sip of white wine and sat forward. "Well, Sir, Tom Meacham told me you wanted a lovely place for a special ride for some of your guests. He suggested the mesa. I rode out to take a look."

"And what did you think?"

"I think it's hot, waterless and not that interesting for something that's supposed to be special."

"Did you tell Mr. Meacham this?"

"Not yet. I haven't had a chance. "But I did talk to a few of the other men in the stable and they mentioned a trail leading along the ocean going south. According to them, there's a way down to the beach a few miles from here and an abandoned building on the beach. I think it's worth a look to find out if it's any good. If it is, picture what we could do. For your opening, your staff could come up with a guest list from your other resorts, high rollers with equestrian skills. They could fly in and ride out to this place. Caterers could set up the beach for a night of dining and partying. Really high-end stuff. Picture it. The ocean, torches, a cool breeze, swimming, hammocks…"

"And ride home the next day with a hangover?" Alberto Montega said, his deep voice full of skepticism.

Elle turned her charm on him. "Oh, no, Mr. Montega. Staff from the resort would bring the horses back. The guests would be flown out in seaplanes. My degree is in public relations. I think we could advertise the hell out of it." She looked back at Alazandro, fluttered her long lashes and added, "The beach is part of your property."

"It would cost a fortune," Montega said dismissively.

"Wealthy people like to spend money on exclusive things. We could repeat it whenever we wanted, plus we could make sure the trail was available as guided rides for other guests. For a price."

Montega opened his mouth.

Alazandro beat him to it with a peal of laughter. "You're going right over Tom Meacham's head," he said.

She looked down at her hands. "I'm sorry. I just got enthusiastic—"

"Don't apologize," Alazandro said. "You have drive and ambition and a pretty face. Meacham has none of those qualities. Okay, you ride out tomorrow and research this."

Elle said, "I thought maybe one of the men could go. I wanted to spend some time with you." As she spoke, she ran a bare foot up his leg and bit her full bottom lip.

Brother, could she be more obvious?

Alazandro said, "I have meetings all day tomorrow. You're the one with the idea, you go research it. Take Meacham. It'll do him good to see how a go-getter works."

Pete stood abruptly. "Maybe I should accompany Ms. Medina," he said.

Alazandro held up a hand. "Meacham will do fine."

"Meacham is a lousy shot," Pete said, "and those trails are unknown to us. Who knows who or what is out there."

Elle fixed him with a stare. "I know how to shoot a gun, remember? I can take care of myself."

Alazandro chuckled. "Split the difference. Take Jorge." Pushing himself away from the table with his good arm, he added, "Alberto, stay the night. We'll finish this discussion in the morning. Right now, I'm taking Ms. Medina for a swim in my private pool. You and Pete get lost."

Pete glanced at Elle, sure he would find her gloating. Instead he found her gazing toward the sea.

Flirty Elle had flown the coop. This Elle was younger and touched his heart in a way he knew from experience meant one thing and one thing only: trouble.

He just wasn't sure why.

"WHERE DID YOU GET this beautiful tattoo?" Elle asked, tracing the dark lines that decorated Alazandro's uninjured bicep.

He'd had the maid fetch her bathing suit from her suite when she refused to swim nude. She knew she'd disappointed him by claiming shyness, but there was no way in the world she was going to laze around Víctor Alazandro's very secluded pool without so much as a scrap of Lycra between herself and his lecherous eyes and hands.

He'd abandoned the sling though he favored the heavily bandaged arm.

"I've had it for years," Alazandro said. "It's my trademark. Doesn't it look familiar to you?" He turned his arm just so.

Elle studied it with a frown before enlightenment came. "It's the same sun as in the mosaic on the front of the resort, right?"

"Smart girl."

"How unique," she gushed and, leaning over, kissed the faded dye. He raised her chin and kissed her. She made herself return the kiss. She'd never dreamed it would be so difficult to flirt with a man she didn't like and though she did her best to be playful and good company, she couldn't get his words out of her mind. *One cop dead, another cop out to get me.*

Her father dead, the judge out to get the murderer.

Alazandro's advances were stilled for a while as a maid served dinner poolside. Elle, reluctant to bring up Seattle again so soon, heard herself saying, "Mr. Alazandro, Víctor, tell me about Amber."

He looked up from his steak. "How do you know about Amber?"

"I heard someone mention her. She died here a couple of months ago, right?"

"She was a mixed-up kid."

"Someone said she overdosed on drugs," Elle persisted. She wondered if Alazandro was still connected to drugs like he had been all those years ago in Seattle—

"People like to gossip," Alazandro said. He looked at the steak, frustrated, as though hacking meat into pieces was beyond his one-handed skills. Putting aside his knife, he took a swallow of red wine. "She brought prescription drugs with her from the States. I'd rather not talk about her."

"Then we won't," Elle said with a smile.

After dinner, Alazandro switched to champagne. Elle took over the pouring duties, filling his flute four times for every one of hers, dumping hers in the pool when he wasn't looking. She acted tipsy and giggly while he held his liquor like a pro until he just seemed to collapse on the lounge next to her.

Elle's sigh mixed frustration with relief as she shifted his weight off her legs. She stood and stared down at him. He'd be so easy to tug over to the rail. One push, a scream of shock from her, her family avenged.

But she didn't know for sure. She hadn't been able to get him to talk about Seattle. She needed him to gloat.

Instead of heaving him over the rail, she pulled him to his feet and guided him to his bedroom. He seemed to rally, grabbing for her as he sat on the edge of the mattress. She fell on top of him, expecting the worst, but his hands slid away from her body. She got to her feet. He was out like a light. All the movement had caused his wound to bleed through the bandage a little. *Nice touch...*

Averting her gaze, Elle quickly tugged off his bathing trunks and covered him with a sheet, messing the linens and denting the pillow on the other side as though they'd had a wild time. She stripped off her own bathing suit and left it in a heap atop of his. The maid had taken Elle's jeans and other clothes to clean and press for morning, so she wrapped herself in the yellow dress and left the apartment.

She giggled at the guard—someone different, not Pete, not the Asian guy. "He's fast asleep," she said with a wide smile as though she'd just had the time of her life and not the longest day in the history of the world.

It was close to ten o'clock as she entered the courtyard. Since so many of the people who worked at the resort lived on the premises, the kitchen ran until midnight. She'd heard Alazandro telling Alberto Montega the current cooks, a local mother-daughter team, would be replaced by a world-famous chef when the place formally opened.

Music poured out of the open windows while voices and laughter wafted on the gentle breeze. Elle walked slowly, barefoot and relaxed, glad to be away from Alazandro though frustrated she'd found out nothing more. Every once and awhile, she'd hear a peal of laughter and smile to herself.

A new noise grew louder as she advanced through the courtyard. She finally identified the sound as splashing water, and veered toward the pool. They must have finished filling it. The fountain would be working.

Glimpsed at first through the oasis of trees and flowers, the three frolicking horses seemed to leap out of the water. Spray shot up between and around their bodies, falling back to drip from manes, backs and flying tails. The underwater pool lights weren't on, but floodlights had been positioned upward to showcase the sculpture. It was stunning.

She walked up close to admire it. The base was bigger than it had been before. Darker. It took her a moment to realize something was caught under the horses' bronze hooves.

She quickly walked around the pool to the other deeply shadowed side. As she walked, her heart froze in place. Not a some*thing*. A some*one*.

She stopped walking, hand covering her mouth, gaze glued to the sight of a tall figure wedged into place, face upturned, water splashing and obscuring his features, one arm trailing in the water, hand floating—

She whispered, "Pete?" and kept moving, straining for a better view of the man's face, a scream lurking in her throat like a pile of kerosene-soaked twigs awaiting the spark of a match.

She gasped as two strong hands clamped down on her arms from behind. A cloth crammed in her mouth cut short a scream. What smelled and felt like a burlap bag was yanked over her head and half her body. Her arms were pinned to her sides with a few rounds of rope pulled tight, her ankles wrapped next.

All this happened in a confused and terrifying blur before she was thrust across someone's shoulder and toted across the courtyard like a bag of feed. She tried to kick and squirm her way free but she might as well have been a mouse trying to escape the clutches of an eagle.

The sound of an engine turning over startled her. Was she within seconds of disappearing into a vehicle? The next destination might be the bottom of the sea or even something worse. Who would do something like this to her?

She knew she had to act fast, but bagged and bound and muffled, what could she do but kick with bare feet?

The abductor's pace picked up. She was thrown onto a hard, vibrating surface that felt like the bed of a truck. Something big and scratchy landed on top of her. She heard yelling and the sound of footsteps running toward her, and for a second her heart swelled with hope. But then a door slammed and she realized there would be no rescue, it was up to her. Launching herself as hard as she could, she rolled over as the vehicle took off. Flying through the air, she landed with a sickening thump that shook her head to toe.

Still gagged and bound, dizzy, wrapped up like a mummy in what she now realized must be an old blanket, she didn't know which way to try to roll next or even if she could. If she'd fallen on a road, she could be run over by the next car. If someone had seen her exit the truck, they'd be back....

A startled grunt was quickly followed by hands grabbing her again. She was lifted, but this time carried in protective arms. Within a few moments, she felt herself lowered gently to the ground.

"It's me," Pete said, but she already knew that. She'd known it the moment he touched her. He lifted her legs and pulled her free from the blanket.

"Damn," he swore, and she felt him struggling with the knots on the rope. "Hold on, I've got a pocket knife," he mumbled, and after a few seconds, she felt tugging. "Damn thing is dull," he said, but he kept sawing until the ropes fell away. He pulled the burlap sack from over her head and their eyes met in the dim light.

As she tired to get the feeling back in her hands, he plucked the gag from her mouth. It had literally drawn every drop of moisture and her tongue stuck to it for an unpleasant second.

And then he cupped her cheeks, searching her eyes. "My, God, Elle. Are you okay?"

She nodded as tears stung the back of her nose and filled her eyes. Her nose started running as he cut her ankles free. And then he pulled her against his chest. Swallowing hard, she whispered, "Jorge," next to his ear.

He held her away, his gaze scanning her face again, his thumbs wiping the tears that trailed down her cheeks. Licking her lips, she added, "In the pool. Caught in the fountain. I think he's...dead."

Pete got to his feet, pulling her up with him. She couldn't believe how wobbly her legs felt. He started to lift her again, but she shook her head. "I can walk," she said and proved it by stumbling. When she took a look around, she found they were close to the patio area that housed the gaily colored carts though some of the overhead lights were broken. She gazed out at the dark road, abandoned now, no sign of the drama that had taken place just minutes before.

He kicked the blanket, sack and rope away, then put his arm around her. "What happened?" he asked as he led her from the portico.

"I saw Jorge under the fountain," she said as they walked. "At first I thought it was you. Then someone grabbed me from behind. Where did you come from?"

"I was hanging out by your place to see if Alazandro talked more about his plans. I heard a scream by the pool area. By the time I got there, you were nowhere in sight, but I did see movement down this way. I got here right as two men threw something into the back of the truck. I hollered at them to stop, but the light was so poor I couldn't see who I was trying to hit. The guy knocked me down and ran off. Before I could pursue him, the truck started to move and the next thing I knew, cargo came flying out and rolled damn near to my feet. The truck raced away without taillights."

She looked up at his face and for the first time noticed the scratches on his left cheekbone. "When I saw the yellow dress and realized it was you—" He stopped short.

She squeezed his hand. "Thank goodness you came. Is there any way to tell who drove off?"

"I'll ask around, but I doubt anyone saw anything. For all we know, they circled around the stable and never even left the premises. There are a dozen different trucks on the grounds. Most have keys tucked under the visor."

"Pete, why would anyone kill Jorge? What's going on?"

Pete paused for a minute before saying, "I don't know. Not for sure."

"But you suspect something?"

"Someone," he said. It was a nonanswer and left Elle as confused as everything else.

They approached the pool from the direction in which Elle had been headed when abducted. The sprinklers had come on, making it impossible to tell if a wet body had been dragged from the pool. The bronze horses still splashed playfully, but there was no sign of Jorge squeezed under their hooves. "Maybe you only thought you saw—"

"No," she said softly. "I saw Jorge. Eyes open, staring without blinking. Dead."

"I don't know what to make of this," Pete said.

Elle had been searching the area around the pool, dodging sprinklers. She saw no dead body stuffed under a piece of furniture or laid out under a bush.

"Let's get inside and talk," Pete said. She took a step toward her suite, but he called her back. "No way. You're not going back there tonight."

"I'm not?"

He spoke as he took her hand. "They had a burlap sack, Elle. Who carries around a sack in the middle of the night? And then they took Jorge's body away. This was planned and you were a target." He swore under his breath before adding, "You're spending the night with me."

For a second, she paused as she glanced around the courtyard at all the waving shadows. The restaurant was still open, the night air still carried the sound of music and voices loud enough, she supposed, to have covered her garbled scream. Loud enough to have covered Jorge's murder and the removal of his body.

"Okay," she said.

PETE QUESTIONED ELLE AGAIN about the kidnapping attempt before moving on to the content of her conversation with Alazandro after he'd sent Pete and Alberto Montega away. She had little to say about either event. He finally handed over his gun and waited until she locked the door. He walked down to the stables, shotgun in hand.

A few men ambled around the stable giving last-minute treats to the horses. Tom Meacham's office was closed and locked. Pete found a group of men in the indoor arena, sitting around a card table they'd drug onto the packed dirt, drinking beer and playing poker.

"*Buenas noches*," he said casually. When they all looked up, he added, "*¿Donde está Jorge?*"

But no one knew where Jorge was and Pete gave up after a while. He walked on down to the gate and talked to one of the men there. No one had seen or heard anything unusual. After making sure no additional shipments of horses were coming through that night, he gave the order to lock the gate for the night.

As he walked back to his place, he thought about what had happened. Why Elle? Unless she had brought trouble with her and he kind of doubted it, then her only worth was to get to Alazandro.

Was it a coincidence that the attack happened on the night Alberto Montega had stayed? Alazandro had made a point of claiming Elle as his property in front of Montega. That wild kiss and the way he'd sent everyone but her away. What if Montega was behind the attacks on

Alazandro's bodyguards and now on Elle? Montega worked for Ciro Ramos. Ciro Ramos had a big operation down in Mexico City. Everyone knew there was no honor between thugs.

But why kill Jorge?

And was Elle still in danger? He picked up his pace and all but ran to his room, knocking lightly on his door so as not to scare her. When she didn't answer, he used his key and opened the door slowly, the shotgun ready.

She'd fallen asleep where he left her. He shut the door, laid the shotgun on the table, and crossed the room, sure she would sense his presence and wake up.

He stood looking down at her for a moment. Dress dirty and torn, hair mussed, dark circles under her eyes, faint bruising on arms and legs—she'd had quite a night. And though it should be the least of his concerns, it was the thought of what had happened with her and Alazandro after he left that afternoon that made him antsy. They'd spent hours together. He stifled a pang of jealousy he had no right to feel, that might mean disaster for both of them if he allowed what was behind it to blossom.

How long had he known her? Two days? Three? You can't grow attached to a person in that short of time. What he felt was lust, nothing more.

She didn't wake when he checked to make sure the safety on the gun was on before he took it from her hand. He was straightening up when her breathing suddenly changed. From under closed lids, her eyes moved side to side. The slackness of sleep gave way to tension. She made a crying sound, her hands rose from her body as though to push something away.

He touched her shoulder. "No!" she screamed. A pitiful scream, a child's voice. She sat bolt upright.

"Elle?"

With a gasp, her eyes fluttered open.

"Are you okay?"

She licked her lips and looked confused.

"Bad dream?"

Swallowing, she nodded, her hands pressed together.

He backed up a couple of steps, not trusting himself. Her defenses were down. His feelings were all over the map.

"Good night," he said and left the room before he did something stupid.

Chapter Nine

"For all intents and purposes, Jorge has disappeared," Pete told Alazandro very early the next morning. He'd spent half the night awake and been up at dawn looking over the pool area. He'd walked Elle to her suite, waited while she showered and put on jeans. They'd shared a silent breakfast of toast and fruit in the resort café, then he'd escorted her to the nice, busy barn where a dozen men who took very little guff from anyone could keep an eye on her. He'd asked her to saddle two horses. One way or another, he was going with her today.

"No one has seen him?" Alazandro said, taking a bite of sausage.

"No one. Elle saw him by the pool last night. Unconscious."

Alazandro's dark eyes flashed at the sound of Elle's name. He was without a sling today, though it was obvious his arm bothered him. "What was she doing by the pool?" he barked. "Frankly, I was…disappointed…. She wasn't here this morning when I woke up."

Pete shook his head. He didn't know why she wasn't here and he didn't care. Okay, that wasn't the truth but it was close. Or it should be. "She was on her way home.

Wanted clean clothes or something. By the way, someone tried to abduct her last night."

"What!"

"I heard something and went to look. She was being tossed into a truck. She…managed to escape."

"Did you get a look at the abductor's faces? A license plate number? Anything?"

"No. It was dark—"

"Can she identify them?"

"No."

"Where is she now?

"Saddling up. Insists on going on that ride today to scout out the trail leading south to the beach."

"Tell her I forbid it. She's safer on these grounds, behind these fences."

"Are we sure about that?" Pete said carefully. "She had all that supposed protection last night and yet—"

"Yes. Where were you, Pete? Isn't that your job, to protect me and my guests?"

"You sent me away," Pete said before he could think of a more diplomatic way of phrasing himself. He spread his hands, affected an ingratiating smile and added, "I'll do whatever you say." *Like hell I will.*

"Then send her over here."

Pete nodded curtly, walked halfway to the door and stopped, turning around slowly as though an idea had just occurred to him. "Maybe you could ride with her."

"The doctor says I can't ride for a week."

Pete knew that. He'd talked to the doctor. He said, "Oh, that's right. You're meeting with Alberto Montega today, anyway." He knew Alazandro was unlikely to allow Elle within a half mile of any kind of meeting, but if he did, maybe he'd allow Pete, as well.

Alazandro put down his juice glass. "I forgot about that. Ramos might stop by, as well."

Ciro Ramos was coming here? Both Ramos and Montega? Now, this was interesting. Pete's face remained impassive as his brain made eager leaps: something was finally beginning to break. This might be it. He'd hunker down here today and keep his mouth shut and his ears open. Maybe one of Ramos' men would let something slip.

When he realized the silence had stretched on too long, he added, "With Jorge missing, maybe it would be better if Elle stayed in her room. We could post a guard or two."

Alazandro said, "And treat her like a prisoner? Not the way to a woman's heart or any other part of her, amigo."

"Maybe not, but she'd be safe," Pete said. She'd also be furious but that couldn't be helped.

"Let her take her little ride," Alazandro said. "I could use the information she's so anxious to gather. It'll make her feel important. Get someone else to go with her."

After the attempt on her made the night before and the questionable situation surrounding Jorge's disappearance? With both Ramos and Montega here? Nope. Pete wasn't about to send Elle off into the wilderness with anyone but himself. He had a choice to make.

"Why don't I go with her? She's comfortable with me. She won't assume I'm guarding her and take off somewhere. I've set things up so you'll be well covered. I'll tell Shen Kuai to stick to you like glue. Ramos will bring his own contingency and I'll be back before dark."

Alazandro thought for a moment. With a shrewd nod, he finally said, "Maybe it would be best if she was with you. Truth is I was a little too drunk to remember much of last night. I want her returned in good condition for tonight." This comment was followed by a lewd wink.

Pete forced a chuckle. "I'll have her back in time for your…plans. Just let me give the place a last once-over before I leave."

Alazandro waved Pete away. Pete sauntered up the stairs and out by the pool where he found a pink bikini and a pair of men's swim trunks draped over lounge chairs as though to dry. Probably the maid's work. He forbid himself to contemplate why Elle left this place without her bathing suit, wearing a dress that wasn't hers.

Up on the roof, he took a good look around to make sure things were secure and that he was alone. When he was sure no one was near, he pulled up his shirt and untaped his new recorder. He'd taken possession of it during a transfer at the hotel when another undercover agent posing as hotel staff delivered a room service breakfast. This was the first chance he'd had to trade out machines.

Pete popped out the old voice-activated micro recorder he'd planted inside a false wall of the wet bar weeks before during his first visit. The unit went in his pocket to be given to his contact in Las Brisas where it would then find its way back to the States. Maybe the lab could weed out background noise. The new gizmo went in its place. The transfer took less than three minutes.

On his way back to the stairs, he eyed the CD player. For a moment, he considered pitching it off the roof, but kept on walking. Why bother? Alazandro would just find another.

Alazandro was just finishing his breakfast as Pete re-entered the room. "Everything looks good, sir. What do you want to do about Jorge?"

"What about him?"

"If Elle's right, the man was unconscious—"

"No doubt dead drunk."

"And Elle's abduction?"

"You can't think of a reason why a couple of these guys might want to make off with a beautiful girl like Elle Medina?"

"Sure. I can also assume if these things keep happening, someone is going to leak it to the media and there goes the resort's grand opening."

Alazandro threw his napkin down next to his plate and thumped a few fingers against the tabletop. Pete would have given a bundle to be inside this guy's head. Here he was, a successful entrepreneur who also ran a drug cartel. The resorts laundered the drug money, especially north of the border. He wanted publicity, in fact he craved it, and yet his dirty drug dealings demanded secrecy. Until now, he'd thought he had both within the walls of this enclave. Now he must be feeling its vulnerability.

"Jorge was skimming wages," Alazandro said. "Maybe the other men got even with him. I should have fired him a long time ago."

As Pete walked away, he considered Alazandro's parting comment.

Why hadn't Alazandro fired Jorge a long time ago?

FOR ELLE, getting away from the resort felt like taking that first gulp of fresh air after being underwater for too long. She welcomed the sun and the white mare's rolling gait as much as she welcomed the fact that Pete rode behind her.

She couldn't tell if Pete believed her or not about Jorge being dead. She'd rerun the memory through her mind a million times and it always played back the same way. Jorge, eyes open, water splattering on his face.

Dead.

So, how long had the abduction and her escape taken? Not more than ten minutes. At most fifteen or twenty. In that time, while she was being carried across the court-yard like a sack of oats, Jorge's body had to have been dislodged from the fountain, tugged to the side of the pool, lifted out and made to vanish.

How?

She looked over her shoulder. Pete looked great astride his horse, hat tipped low over his forehead, shirt sleeves rolled up bare muscular arms. "I asked about Jorge down at the stable this morning," she said. "No one has seen him since dinner last night. A couple of the guys hinted he wasn't coming back."

"Who?"

"I don't know their names. But the bracket supporting the water bucket in one of the stalls is twisted and bent."

He straightened up a little. "Maybe it's been bent for weeks."

"No, it's in the stall I use to go in and out of the barn. I'd have noticed it before this. Maybe Jorge wasn't drowned in the pool. The thought of someone holding his head in that bucket—"

"I'll take a look at it when we get back," Pete said.

The first half of the ride took them toward Las Brisas. Pete insisted they stop for cold drinks. He disappeared inside a very dusty looking gas station while she stayed with the horses. Through the smudged front window, she saw him talking to a man as he opened an old ice chest and took out a couple of bottles of water, paying the man and reappearing in moments. Since they had water in their saddlebags, she wasn't sure why they'd taken the diversion, but there was no doubting the cold water felt like ambrosia as it washed down her throat.

They were soon off again, regaining the trail. The footing was good as it followed the lazy river out of town and toward the sea.

With the ocean sparkling to their right, the trail gradually began sloping toward the beach far below. It wasn't long before they were making a series of hairpin turns as they descended. The vegetation increased and the ocean disappeared and reappeared as they wound their way down the hillside. It was very quiet.

They paused a few hundred feet above the beach, pulling their horses to a halt on a jutting curve in the trail. They sat side by side as the sun beat down on their backs. The vast ocean stretched out to the horizon.

"I see the building," Elle said, leaning forward on her saddle.

Pete put out a hand as if to catch her. She smiled at him and he laughed. "It's just that you're kind of close to the edge there, Elle. If that horse spooks, you and he are both going to end up on the rocks below."

She looked straight down at the rocks. She *was* close to the edge and she urged the horse to take a few steps backward.

Pete was right, a person would die if they fell from this spot. Now she had three possible places to exterminate Alazandro if that's what it came to.

Pete said, "Elle? Where'd you go? You look like you're a million miles away."

She blinked a few times. "Let's see if this is all as nice as it looks."

The footing got trickier, the trail needed improving in spots, but their horses were surefooted. She made mental notes as though she really was doing a job because maybe she was wrong, maybe Alazandro was just what he appeared to be—a highly successful and egotistical businessman with a death threat hanging over his head and a tendency to do things his way. A scapegoat for the Seattle police who had had nothing to do with her family's deaths, a man who had turned his life around, who had made something of himself.

Pete had told her Alazandro wanted her again that night and the look in his eyes as he'd said it let her know he thought he knew exactly what was going on. Tonight she had to get Alazandro to talk about Seattle. She thought she knew how.

The sound of the surf grew louder as they descended. They finally made the beach and walked the horses along the coarse sand until they reached a lush grove of palms. A small spring bubbled into a shallow pool. They took the saddles off the horses, tethered them to a rope Pete strung between two of the trees and let them drink their fill.

"I want to see what the building looks like," Elle said. As they approached it, Elle could see that, though it needed work, it held a sort of faded charm highlighted by weathered white paint and green shudders hanging lopsided. Some of the windows were broken and the double front doors were missing. The metal roof needed patching. There was no plumbing or power, so the building's original purpose remained unclear. Inside, it was one big open space, mostly sound, cluttered only by debris brought inside during storms.

The porch was broad and long, covered by an extension of the roof. They sat for a moment, hot and sweaty from the ride.

Pete said, "Maria packed us a lunch. Are you hungry?"

"Not yet," Elle said. "This is so beautiful."

"Want to walk down near the water?"

"Sure."

They got up and trudged down the beach until it ended at the southern-most end in a rocky point. "I wish I'd brought my suit," Elle said, plopping down on the sand. It was high tide and the sea broke against the rocks. As well as a sense of privacy, the place provided a bit of welcome shade. She pulled off her boots and socks and wiggled her toes. Pete stood looking down at her, his back to the sea. His eyes were the color of the water behind him.

"You left your suit at Alazandro's place," he said as he yanked off his boots and socks, too, hopping from one foot to the other. He unbuckled the shoulder strap and handed it and the gun to Elle as he stripped off his shirt, exposing his lightly tanned and muscular chest, a dusting of curly hair bleached by the sun. He was a tall man, lanky in build, and she hadn't expected so many muscles.

She gave him back the gun and holster. With a blue-eyed sweep of the hills behind them, he laid it on his discarded shirt to protect it from the sand. He stood over her again, half naked, so strong and ruggedly good looking she couldn't turn away.

She took his hand and pulled. He fell to his knees between her bent knees. "What happened last night?" he asked. "At Alazandro's place."

She shook her head. "Not much. I told you—"

"Are you sure?"

"Pete—"

"Just tell me."

She leaned forward and touched his lips with hers. "Ask him, why don't you," she whispered.

"He says he was drunk. He says he doesn't remember."

She smiled inwardly as she said, "Well, there was a lot of champagne. It was easy to overindulge."

"You weren't drunk. I was with you minutes after you left and you were stone sober."

"A kidnapping attempt sobers a woman right up," she said as his mouth drifted closer.

She tried to tell herself this wasn't a good idea, but it felt like a perfect idea and she was honest enough with herself to admit she'd been wanting it since the moment they hit the beach.

His lips, warmed by the sun, devoured hers. He pushed her down on her back and she tugged him along with her.

How could she go from thinking about pushing a man off a cliff to desiring another within the same hour? What was wrong with her? Would she ever be the same again? Would Pete still want to look at her if he knew what she was thinking about?

Her distraction must have showed, for Pete pushed himself away a little. Still more or less on top of her, he rested his weight on his forearms, his head above hers. "What's going through that agile brain of yours, Elle Medina?" he asked, smoothing a strand of hair away from her eyes.

"You don't want to know," she said softly.

"Yes, I do," he said. "I want to know all about you. You must know that by now."

"You do know all about me," she insisted. "You've done the background search and you've looked through my belongings. I have no secrets left."

"You have two," he said. "Correction, you have two I know of."

"Just two? Okay. But I go first."

He smiled. Man, when he did that his angular face just lit up. His eyes glistened. His lips were full and inviting. She was his for the taking at that moment—thankfully, he didn't seem to understand the pull of his magnetism. He said, "Okay, ask away."

"What did you do before you became a bodyguard for Alazandro?"

"Easy. I was a soldier and then a cop. Alazandro is under the impression I went to prison, so please, don't tell him. It'll ruin my tough-guy image. Next?"

"Tell me about your last girlfriend."

"My last girlfriend? Well, frankly, she was a drug addict, the sister of an old friend of mine from the force. The man took a bullet for me so I looked up his sister when I got back. We stayed in and out of touch for years."

"Was she your...lover?"

"At first. But not the last time we hooked up. Let's just say she was pretty creative in the ways she chose to finance her drug habit. I'd have had to have been crazy."

"And you're not crazy."

"No," he said with a half smile that tugged at Elle's heart. Alazandro had been involved with drugs years before, had been a small-time dealer according to police records. Apparently he'd gone straight after he left Seattle. Did Pete know he was working for someone like that? If he did, would he care? He'd made it clear he was in this for the money.

He just didn't seem like the kind of guy who dedicated his life to following money. But then, sometimes people couldn't afford to be choosy.

"She died earlier this year," he added. "I have since given up needy women. Maybe that's why I'm so attracted to you."

"Because I'm not needy," she said.

"No. You're just mysterious. I've given up one pain-in-the-neck kind of woman for another."

She smiled. "Are you close to your family? Is your last name really Waters?"

"More questions. You're not very good at math, are you?"

"Humor me."

"Okay, what else would my last name be? Parents divorced. Dad is remarried. Mom plays the field. My little sister has two kids, no current husband. Brother married, one kid. They'll all love you."

She started to laugh, but then the import of his words hit her heart like a sledgehammer and it was all she could do not to turn her head. By embracing vengeance as a viable course of action, she'd turned her back on normal relationships. She saw this now in a way she hadn't before. By promising her grandfather she'd make sure her dead family could finally rest in peace, no matter how obscure and specious a plan, she'd forgone peace for herself.

"My turn," he said, nudging her chin back in his direction with his forefinger. His eyes delved deep into hers.

The sun seemed to dip behind a cloud, but that was just an illusion, that was just his head blocking the sun as the sun chased the shade across the sand. "There are at least two of you in there," he said. "The funny, smart aleck was here a few moments ago but now she's gone. Fled in an instant."

"I take it back. You are crazy," she said.

"No I'm not. One minute you're a sexy temptress and the next you're a kid. You go from scheming to breezy faster than a speeding bullet. Which one is real?"

She bit at her top lip, not sure what to say. Was she that obvious, and if she was, did Alazandro see right through her?

"Second question," he said, resetting his weight a little. His body lay atop hers, his heat overpowering her, intoxicating her. His voice was soft and low, the nearby surf almost drowning out his words. He lowered his head until his lips were next to her ear. The feel of his warm breath caressing her lobe sent chills through her body.

"What do you really want with Víctor Alazandro?" he whispered as though he knew her answer was a secret and if she answered softly enough, it would stay there between them.

She pushed on his chest gently and he rolled off her onto his side. Propping his head on his hand, he stared down at her. What did he know about secrets? His life seemed an open book.

She took a deep breath and said, "I want Alazandro to need me so badly he'll advance me within his business without making me wait around."

"Without making you earn your way you mean?"

She took a deep breath and nodded.

He studied her face. She couldn't tell what he thought of her sleazy admission. She really, really didn't like lying to him. He'd been so upfront with her, he deserved better than this.

She thought of the judge. He'd been a father to her, and though not an easy man to get close to, she owed him better than lies and deception. Would she ever have a chance to make up what she owed him?

"What about the two Elle's?"

She looked him in the eye and gave a partial truth. "I've read that children who lose their parents when they're very young carry a child inside for the rest of their life. Maybe you see mine peeking through once in a while. I don't know."

"I don't know, either," he said. He waited a moment before adding, "Did you have sex with Alazandro?"

"No."

"Good."

For a few moments the sound of the sea seemed to recede, the sun seemed to duck behind invisible clouds. For a few moments, there was just him and her and the warm sand.

She touched his face. Electricity jumped from his skin into her fingertips and she blinked. She ran her fingers along his firm jaw, over his ear, keeping her touch as light as a feather. His hair was short, no long strands through which to run her fingers. No-nonsense hair.

"Elle—"

"Don't talk," she whispered or she thought she did, she honestly couldn't hear her own voice. The silence that had descended around them in that eerie way had been supplanted by a roaring inside her head, fueled by the thunderous pumping of her heart.

She put her lips against his lips. And that was the match that lit the fuse.

For Elle, the touch of his lips was like a call home, a new sensation that rocked her deep inside. She put a hand around his neck and pulled him close, parting her lips to accept the exploration of her mouth by his tongue, her body arcing toward his, aching for his touch.

He kissed her for a long time before his fingers trailed down her body and under her shirt, around to her bra. With one nimble movement, he'd unhooked the little clasp in the front and freed her breasts from their satin cover. His hands explored her flesh in a gentle but demanding way that claimed ownership of her body. The time to reclaim it was right this instant. Either that or let it go.

With one arm, he lifted her head, pulled off her shirt and bra, interrupting their kisses for only a second. Bare skin pressed against bare skin and the heat of his chest against her breasts as his hands tugged at her jeans turned her inside out.

With almost frantic anxiety, they rose to their feet and stripped each other of their remaining clothes. For a second they looked at each other. Elle had never seen such a beautiful man and her lust for him overcame any remaining shy bones she still possessed. She touched him and he moaned, and with that touch she claimed ownership over him, at least for this little while.

They fell back to the sand in a tangle of arms and legs, kisses hot and wet, hands exploring the contours of each other's willing bodies. Elle pulled him on top of her and closed her eyes against the brilliance of the day as he plunged inside her, his need as volatile as her own.

Under the wide blue Mexican sky, he made love to her in a way she'd never been made love to before. If, during the three times they sought affirmation and release, it crossed her mind that this was not a wise thing to do, that this added layers of complications she couldn't afford, she pushed the thought aside for another time, another day.

For this one moment, she let go of hate.

Chapter Ten

Pulling her to her feet, Pete said, "How about a swim?" and took off.

Elle almost caught up with him by the time they hit the warm water. The surf roiled over their knees as they faced it head on. He grabbed her hand and, turning sideways as the waves continued to come, they plowed their way through one by one. Elle's heart seemed to swell every time the powerful waves lifted her off her feet until they were beyond the surf.

She didn't know how long they floated and dived. She just knew she felt free in a way she hadn't for a long time, at one with herself, with a man she cared for deeply, with the ocean. The overhead sun was surely taxing her heavy-duty sunscreen, but she didn't care. She was in the moment, with no past and no future. And, for a while, it seemed she could stay this way, she didn't have to go back, she didn't have to become someone and something she wasn't.

A playful tug pulled her under. She splashed her way back up, breaking the surface a moment before Pete did. His grin filled her head with possibilities.

"Your nose and shoulders are pink," he said, paddling close enough to plant a salty, wet kiss on her lips.

"Thanks to rolling out of the truck last night, the rest of me is black and blue."

"No one wears a bruise like you do," he said, and glancing up at the sun, added, "We'd better get back."

She didn't want to go back, but she allowed herself to be coaxed toward the breakers. They rode a wave in close to the shore, waded through the sand, then stood together for a moment, looking at the white beach, him standing behind her, his arms wrapped around her waist as sea water washed around their calves.

Maybe this was a turning point. Maybe she was ready to find a way to let go...

She said, "Pete? What's going on back at the resort?"

"You mean with Jorge missing?"

"I mean everything. Is it all connected to whoever is trying to get Alazandro?"

"I don't know," he said. "Some of it seems to be, but I don't see why anyone would murder Jorge. All the same, just to be on the safe side, don't be alone with Montega."

"Why?"

"I don't trust him."

"How about Tom Meacham? He didn't like Jorge much."

"Don't be alone with anyone except me," he said. "From now on there'll be someone in Alazandro's apartment at all times."

She felt a trickle of alarm. How was she going to pump Alazandro if someone else was always around?

And following the alarm, a profound sense of relief for the very same reason. It seemed everything was conspiring to give her a back door, a way out....

She said, "Everyone who comes to see Mr. Alazandro seems armed to the teeth. Why?"

"He's told them all about the death threat," Pete said, looking past her shoulder, out to sea.

"Who are the 'they,' anyway? I mean, I heard someone named Ciro something or other was coming. Is he a thug like Alberto Montega?"

He looked back into her eyes. "Who told you Ciro Ramos was coming?"

"Tom Meacham. I went by his office to apologize for going over his head about the beach thing. I thought Mr. Alazandro might have told him. He said—no, wait, he wasn't talking to me, he was talking on the phone and I had to wait. He said something like, "Ciro Ramos is due here in a few hours—"

She stopped because Pete had grown very still. "What's wrong, Pete? What is it?"

"When you quoted him just now, you lowered your voice. Did Tom do that, too?"

"Yes."

"As though he didn't want anyone listening?"

"I guess. But you know how his voice carries and the stable was bustling with people. Why? Is it important?"

"I don't know," he said, but he had already started wading back through the surf, pulling her along with him. "We'd better be on our way," he added.

She wanted to tug him back out to deep water or make a nest in the tired old building or pitch a camp near the spring. She wanted to stay here and never go back, never see Alazandro again, never have another nightmare or contemplate murder or lie to Pete, not ever, not for the rest of her life.

Not even for her grandfather.

THEY RODE BACK IN SILENCE. Pete was anxious for a whole host of reasons and while the foremost should be what was going on in that impromptu meeting between Alazandro, Ciro Ramos and Montega, it wasn't.

The bulk of his worries concentrated on the woman riding in front of him. And while a majority of those had to do with how he was going to keep her safe when the bullets started flying, a troubling minority had to do with the fact that he was delivering her back to Alazandro.

Face it, he was jealous. It was unprofessional, pointless, damn near inexcusable. But it was also a fact. He didn't want her around the man. He didn't want her in harm's way. And he knew there was very little he could do to keep her from either. It was just that she didn't know what was going on. Despite her scheming ways, she was so innocent.

It irked him to have so many unanswered questions. To leave at least one suspected murder unsolved, to ignore car chases and gun attacks, all because he had to keep his eye on the bottom line. He hoped the tape he'd passed to Juan at the gas station turned out to be a hell of lot more enlightening than the others had been.

They arrived at the stable to find everyone asking a lot of pointed questions about Jorge, or rather the fact that Jorge still hadn't turned up. Tom Meacham had apparently left the resort in his anxiety to escape talking to the men—made sense to Pete since Tom didn't know much Spanish.

There was no doubt the men were getting a little spooked by Rudy's death and then Jorge's disappearance, though, and while some of them whisked away the tired horses for proper grooming and feeding, the rest peppered Elle with questions and demands.

Pete knew payday was at the end of the week and wondered how many of these guys would stick around afterward. Rumor had it a mad killer was loose.

Pete admired the way Elle listened and promised to talk to Mr. Alazandro about their concerns. He did what he could to assure everyone guards would keep them safe, but the men weren't fools and they all knew the perimeter was huge and bordered by the sea on one side.

There were also horse transports coming and going and thus the strangers who drove and acted as grooms. Other than a thorough search of each transport, how could Pete guarantee no madman was aboard? And even then?

While Elle promised to do what she could, Pete wandered over to Tom's office. As the locked door was made of glass, it was easy to see Tom had left everything in its usual state of chaos.

He looked into the stall Elle had mentioned. The water bucket was missing, a lighter patch of wood showing where it had once been attached.

"It's gone," Elle said.

They both looked around to see if anyone was watching. Pete said, "Vanished. Just like Jorge."

"Pete—"

"Listen. Keep your appointment with Alazandro. And tell me if he mentions any more visitors. I know you've talked to him a lot about Seattle so you could establish what you have in common, but maybe you could talk about other things, like the future or—"

He stopped talking because she was staring at him. "What's wrong?"

She shook her head. "I don't know. For a second, you seemed like someone else. It must be all the sun I've had today."

"Yeah," Pete said, and let the topic drop. He walked her back to her suite and waited while she took a quick shower and changed clothes. In less than twenty minutes, she reappeared in red shorts and a white halter top that set off her cleavage and her sunburned nose. She'd combed damp hair behind her ears.

She looked good enough to eat. Good enough to tote back into her bedroom. He had a horrible sinking feeling that he'd again started something that was going to end badly and he felt alternately like kicking himself and kissing her.

She must have seen the look in his eyes, for she circled him out of arm's reach. "Don't make this harder than it is already," she said.

He stood his ground. "Is it hard?" he asked.

"You know it is."

"So, what would you rather do tonight?"

She smiled as she looked down at the floor. "You know that, too." She put one hand on the knob and paused. Looking back over her shoulder, she said, "Do you ever wish we'd met somewhere else, sometime else?"

"Every day," he said honestly.

She nodded as she opened the door.

He reached out and caught the edge of the door in his hand. Looming over her, he whispered, "Elle, why don't you go home? In a few weeks, I'll be free of this…situation…and I'll join you, wherever you are. I can't make you vice president of anything, but I have other attributes."

"Yes, you do," she whispered in such a way his blood boiled.

"Go home. Please."

She leaned her head against his hand. For the first time

since they'd met, he sensed indecision in her. She looked up at him through the corners of her eyes and said, "I have to admit I'm tempted."

Afraid to say anything lest he push her the wrong way, he stayed quiet.

She added, "I've been thinking today. About my plans, I mean. They're beginning to seem like a bad idea. I've begun to wonder if there isn't another way."

Inside he pumped his arm and shouted *Yes!* Outside, he said, "Oh?"

"I have to talk to Alazandro about the stable hands' concerns. They're scared. If he wants to keep them, he's going to have to come up with a bonus."

"I know," he said, lowering his lips to brush across her forehead. "And then?"

She tilted her head just a little so that their mouths all but touched. The gesture was an invitation. He cupped her jaw, ran his fingers down her throat. Her pulse beneath his fingertips was strong and steady, and his groin burned with desire. His hand swept slowly down her bare arm, his fingers tangling with hers next to her bare thigh. He was one heartbeat away from lifting her off her feet and carrying her back into her bedroom. The beach suddenly seemed as though it had happened months before.

A knock sounded on the partly open door. Pete jerked upright as Elle startled. She yanked the door all the way open to reveal an equally startled looking housekeeper holding a manila folder. As Pete moved away from the door, the maid explained the contents of the folder had just come over the fax machine in the office. Elle thanked her as Pete handed the woman a tip.

Pete watched Elle's face as she turned the sheet of paper inside the folder this way and that until she paused and, right before his eyes, lost about a week's worth of tan.

"Elle?"

She closed the folder. Looking right at him, she blinked a few times as though she'd been so far away she'd forgotten who he was.

"What is it?" he asked.

She shook her head. "Nothing."

"Come on, talk to me. You're upset."

"It's about my…grandfather. I told you he was very ill."

He approached her with the intent of gathering her into his arms. But she withdrew. It's not like she moved or anything, she just kind of shrank and he knew she didn't want him to touch her.

"We'd better go," she said, her hand still clutching the folder like nobody's business.

"Are you taking that with you?"

She looked trapped.

"You can leave it here, Elle. I won't look. It's none of my business, right?"

"It's just medical stuff."

He didn't believe her. He also didn't believe someone had faxed her anything that had to do with his case and so he meant it when he promised to stay away. "I'll wait outside while you hide it somewhere." Without waiting for her reply, he closed the door behind him and waited a few minutes for her to reappear.

He smiled reassuringly at her but he couldn't help notice, from over her shoulder, the wisps of smoke and charred ashes in the stucco fireplace inside her suite. She'd burned what was in the folder. Why would she burn an old man's medical file?

"I'm ready," she said and, without meeting his gaze, started along the path toward the courtyard.

She didn't need to say a word. Her ramrod posture, downcast eyes and preoccupation said it all for her.

Whatever had been in that folder had changed her mind. She was back on track, whatever that track was.

And she was walking away from him.

"YOU MUST MISS YOUR CHILDREN," Elle said as she replaced the framed photo of the four appealing Alazandro kids atop the wet bar. Wanting to bring the subject around to her family, she'd decided to start with his.

Alazandro regarded her from his perch atop the waist-high wall that surrounded the rooftop patio. They'd already been swimming, they'd eaten, they'd ironed out a bonus for the men. Now she was playing a game with very high stakes.

Alazandro had thrown a towel around his neck after swimming.

"I see them twice a year," he said. "Francisco, he's my oldest and my only son, graduates from college next year. He'll come work with me. The girls are young and need to be with their mother still."

"How about your parents?"

"My father died many years ago. My mother is Mexican. Born in Guadalajara. After my sisters and brothers and I grew up, she moved back to Guadalajara to be with her mother."

"How nice," Elle said as though she didn't know all this. "Do you see your grandmother often?"

He shook his head. "Not often. I'm a busy man."

"My grandfather is still alive," she said musingly. "He's very ill, though. In fact, he's dying."

Alazandro heaved a bored sigh and studied his finger-nails. His interest was flagging. She added, "I talked to him this afternoon after I got back from the beach. He recognized your name."

She had his attention. "This surprises you? I'm a well known man, *muñeca.*"

She slithered off the bar stool and sashayed to a stop in front of him, leaning forward over his legs to playfully touch the tip of his nose. That position should give him an eyeful of breasts and keep his mind half occupied.

With a mental apology to her seventy-four year old grandfather, whose memory was sharp as a tack, she said, "Grandpa's memory is shot except for the old days. *Those* he remembers perfectly. He lived in Seattle twenty years ago. He worked on the paper, in fact, he covered the murder investigation of a cop and he remembered your name from back then. It gave him a thrill to recall it all." She touched Alazandro's cheek and gazed into his empty eyes, adding, "He remembers you, specifically."

Alazandro said, "Why would he remember me?"

"I told you, he was a reporter, he covered the story. He mentioned the cop's family was murdered, too. He said you knew the cop. I told him he must be mistaken."

For a second, she thought she'd gone too far. Even the breeze seemed to hold its breath....

Alazandro finally said, "*Tu abuelo* is crazy."

Pressing her barely covered bust against Alazandro's arm, she purred, "That's what I told him. More or less."

His gaze strayed down her body, lingering at hip level. She said, "You're so tense. Why don't I give you a massage?"

"I can think of a better way for you to help me with tension," he said, patting her rear end.

"What's the hurry?" she said with a smile. She moved to a chair, motioned at the seat and said, "Come on, I'm really good at this. I'll be careful of your arm."

He did as she asked, settling into the chair with a sigh. She stood behind him massaging his shoulders. After a minute or two, she said, "So, you never met the murdered cop?"

He caught her hand and pressed it against his lips. "Why do you keep asking about this cop?"

She kept her voice soft as she said, "Are you kidding? It's exciting. Sexy, even."

He laughed. "To humor you, then, okay. No, I never met the man."

"Grandpa said there was an envelope with a fingerprint found at the house—"

"The so-called evidence. It disappeared," he said, and she could *hear* the smile in his voice. "They had nothing on me."

She took an even bigger chance and said, "The murder of the wife and the baby, though. That was shocking."

He released her hand. With an impatient jerk of his head, he growled, "Trust me, the woman and child died in their sleep, they had no idea what happened to them. They died peacefully. Only the man knew what was coming. And he got what he deserved."

"That's a cold way to look at it," she said, glad he couldn't see her face.

"You're a woman," Alazandro said with a dismissive tone in his voice. "You don't understand."

For the count of ten, she moved her hands rhythmically, kneading his shoulders, while her mind conjured up the images of her dead family. He'd all but admitted he'd killed them.

After the evidence disappeared, the police had had no way to connect Alazandro to the murder scene. They'd had to let him go.

And all the time, the one piece of evidence that would have put him in her house or at least in contact with her father had been right in front of their eyes.

She ran a finger over Alazandro's tattoo. He caught her hand. "You like my sun, don't you?" he said, turning to glance up at her.

"It's unique. Have long have you had it?"

"Fifteen years or sô."

"You said it's your trademark."

"*Sí.* I found the picture in one of my father's books when I was very young. It had a little face in it. I thought it was cool so I made it my own."

"But this doesn't have a face."

"I dropped the face when I moved away from Seattle."

She smiled. Twenty years before, he'd drawn that same stylized sun on a brown envelope, only with a face. The last time she'd seen the envelope, it had been lying close to her father's body. It had apparently held a tape of a drug deal. It had apparently yielded fingerprints belonging to Víctor Alazandro. One of the investigators had reproduced the sun after the envelope went missing, but no one had connected the sun to Alazandro. He hadn't had a tattoo back then; despite his inflated opinion of himself, the police had not known the sun was his trademark.

It took twenty years. Scott's brother, Kevin, had sent the image to Scott on a whim. Scott had faxed it to Elle on another whim. And she had linked it to Alazandro.

"Not so hard, *cariña.* My shoulder hurts."

"Sorry," Elle said automatically, slipping her hands from his shoulders.

"You're distracted. It's usually so peaceful here. But not lately."

"No, not lately," she said.

"No more upsetting talk. Tell me about my beach."

Putting aside her feelings was no easy task. With his words, her fury had bubbled to the surface but she still needed an outright confession before she killed the man. She knew that was the only thing that would make the killing possible for her. Maybe the confession would have to come at gunpoint—

Digging up cool detachment she didn't know she had, she told him about the crescent of sand and palms, adding, "It's going to need work. I'll discuss it with Tom."

"It's your project, not Meacham's." He pulled her around to stand in front of him, patting his legs. "Can you get the place ready in a few weeks' time?"

"All it takes is money," she said as she sat gingerly on his lap.

"You're a fast learner, Elle Medina." His voice had gotten soft and husky as his hand drifted south.

She knew what was coming. His hand roamed up and down her bare leg, edging higher up her thigh each time.

"You're trembling," he said with relish.

If you only knew the half of it…

She'd known getting into this that there would come a time when to achieve what she had to achieve, she might have to participate in a sexual relationship with Alazandro.

As a cacophony of raised voices reached the rooftop, Alazandro's caresses ceased and she took her first breath in what seemed five minutes. They both got to their feet and hurried to the part of the patio that overlooked the second floor.

Pete and another man were halfway up the stairs. Pete, pausing midstep, looked up as though sensing Elle's presence. Their gazes met and in that instant, Elle knew no matter what, she couldn't—she wouldn't—have sex with Víctor Alazandro.

She felt almost faint with relief.

"They found Jorge," Pete said.

ONE OF THE HOUSEKEEPERS and her boyfriend who worked in the kitchen, had gone for a walk on the beach that evening. They'd come across Jorge's battered and lifeless body washed up on the rocks at the base of the cliff.

It was dark now. Elle stood on the bluff, watching the well-lit recovery effort, her arms wrapped around herself. She'd wanted a distraction, but not this. And yet she'd known for twenty-four hours that Jorge was dead.

Pete stood a foot behind her and she longed to take a step back and feel his arms wrap around her.

Pete said, "Have the police talked to you yet?"

"I gave them a statement. I couldn't tell if they believed me when I told them I saw Jorge under the fountain last night." Her voice had a funny, faraway tone. It had started when Alazandro described the way her mother and baby brother died.

The coroner's report said her mother had been shot through the heart from the back. The bullet had exited her body and entered the sleeping infant tucked in beside her. Elle's baby brother, Sammy, dead at four weeks, three days.

Had her mother had a chance to open her eyes to see what had happened to her baby? Had she had a split second to fear what had happened or would happen to her daughter, five year old Elle, known as Janey to her family, playing quietly in her room?

Were their deaths really peaceful? The coroner's report had stated death was instantaneous for both of them, but how did he know?

And how did Alazandro know unless he'd stood there with their blood on his hands and watched them die?

She needed to hear those words from his lips, *I killed them.* She had to hear him say that.

"Elle?"

"I couldn't tell if the police even *wanted* to believe me," she said.

"It does seem everyone wants Jorge's death to be another accident like Rudy's," Pete said, his gaze seemingly directed beyond her, down to the beach.

"You mean Alazandro wants it that way," she said.

"He's worried about bad publicity. And I guess if he isn't the murder victim, he doesn't much care who is."

Elle didn't respond. She'd been relieved when Alazandro sequestered himself with a high-ranking police official in his apartment, sending her away for the night. No awkwardness, no pretend tantrum on her part in order to escape having sex, no chance he'd send her home in disgust.

"So I guess we're supposed to picture Jorge, staggering around so drunk he fell off the cliff and drowned in the ocean," Pete said.

"If he died in the pool or the water bucket, the water in his lungs won't be saltwater," Elle said.

"If anyone checks."

She hugged herself even tighter. It was a warm, humid evening and yet she felt chilled through to the bone.

"Someone here is not who they pretend to be," Pete said softly.

Ambient light glittered in his eyes. If she asked him to run away with her right now, would he?

What would he think if he knew who she really was?

What would it do to him if he had to hurt her to protect Alazandro?

Before he could sense the guilt that did everything but erupt like sparklers from the top of her head, she turned away and gazed out at the black ocean.

Chapter Eleven

"I feel like I've been stuck in this damn apartment for years," Alazandro announced the next morning. "Between your caution and that damn doctor's orders, I'm going stir crazy."

The police had taken Jorge's body away in the dead of night. Pete had taken a quick look, but between the fall and being submerged in the ocean for a day or so, there wasn't much to see in the way of evidence. A decent coroner might find something but it was doubtful if one would be called.

Staring through Alazandro's windows, Pete could see three officers down on the beach using the morning light to search for additional clues. Pete suspected they would find none.

"Elle tells me the men are spooked," Alazandro said.

"They were before this latest incident. I can't imagine what they're feeling now."

"She thinks half of them will bolt once they get paid. I authorized a bonus for every man who stays."

Typical Alazandro, trying to buy his way out of every mess he helped create. Pete said, "I don't know if a bonus is going to be enough to hold them."

"What we need is a fiesta."

Pete did a double take. "Sir?"

"I'll make an appearance and reassure everyone that all is well, we had a couple of accidents is all. We'll make sure there's plenty of tequila."

"It's too dangerous for you to go outside. Jorge—"

"Jorge had nothing to do with me. The men need to see I'm not afraid. We'll have it tonight."

If Pete mentioned his misgivings about Montega and Ramos, would Alazandro bolt? He couldn't chance that. He said, "Are Montega and Ramos still here? Perhaps they'd like to come."

"No, no, they're long gone. We'll hold it out in the courtyard. Invite everyone who can be spared from their regular positions. Get the guys at the airport to come on over, too. Rotate in the guards. Tell the kitchen to cook up a storm, tell Elle to get the place decorated. And get a band. Nothing cheers people up like a band."

Looked to Pete as though he'd been demoted to cruise director... "Sure. What else?"

"Elle will know. Tell her to organize it." Alazandro pushed himself away from the table where he'd been daintily eating French toast as he plotted his impromptu party. He was actually smiling. "Leave Shen Kuai outside my door. I got a call this morning, things are in motion. FYI, I'll be holding an important meeting here the end of the week. You'll need to beef up security."

Pete grew very still inside. *A meeting.* In a casual voice he asked, "So, Ramos and Montega are coming back?"

"Among others. I can't afford to lose half my staff right now. Horses are coming and going. My lawyers report they're in final negotiations with a management candidate. This fiesta has to be enough to make the men rethink abandoning ship. No scandal. Period."

"Sure," Pete said again, excitement banished to the furthest recesses of his mind. "I'll go upstairs and check out your rooftop before you retire up there to make your calls. I assume that's where you'll work today?"

"Probably," Alazandro said, settling on the sofa with the newspaper. "Make it quick."

Pete climbed the stairs two at a time. With a 360 degree glance, he made sure he was alone, then retrieved the tape and put in a new one. Next week! Finally. And he had several days notice.

It was enough to make an undercover agent grin from ear to ear.

AFTER STOPPING BY the main kitchen and alerting the unflappable staff that they had twelve hours to come up with a party menu for two hundred people, Pete walked down to the barn. He made a very hurried call to arrange a drop for the tape and to alert the right people that the anticipated meeting was scheduled for sometime late next week, more information forthcoming.

He hoped.

Man, was this finally the beginning of the end? Was that a glimmer of light up ahead? He would get some names if it killed him. Maybe the tape today would handle that. His government would contact the Mexican government. The guy at the gas station would act as go-between, by this time next week, a horde of international agents would descend on this place, round up ten of the worst thugs in Mexico and hopefully make a dent in this horrible methamphetamine epidemic.

And then, he was out of here. No more undercover

work. That few hours on the beach with Elle had shown him what life could be like with a decent woman who was just a little mixed up. Hell, everyone was just a little mixed up. He was a little mixed up.

Point was, he was crazy about her. He wanted to take her away from all this and for a moment, she'd been willing to consider it. He clung to that. If she'd felt that way once, maybe she would again.

Maybe she'd consent to come to Santa Barbara. If not, he'd go where she was. They needed time, he knew that….

So what was in that folder? Maybe it had something to do with why she was here because he didn't buy that spiel about wanting to be promoted without merit.

The stable was bustling with men leading horses out of stalls and into a transport that had arrived during the night and was taking off again. He left the activity at the far end of the stable as he walked deeper into the interior toward Tom Meacham's office. Pete took a deep breath of relief when he found Tom sitting at his desk.

Pete slid open the door and Tom looked up from his papers.

"Good to see you," Pete said.

Tom scratched his pink head and smiled shyly. "It got too complicated here yesterday."

"So, you took off."

"Seemed a good idea at the time."

"I suppose you heard about Jorge."

"Yeah. Some of the guys are saying he got what he deserved. I don't know, I kind of liked the man. And that pay-skimming thing was way overdone. There was no proof."

Pete narrowed his eyes. After a moment of thought that

revealed nothing to him, he slapped a hand against the wall and said, "I heard you knew Ciro Ramos was coming."

"You did? How?"

"Elle Medina heard you on the phone."

"The little snoop."

It was on the tip of Pete's tongue to protest. Instead, he closed the glass door and turned away. He looked around for Elle and found her in the stall kitty-corner from Meacham's office.

Before he called out, her activity aroused his curiosity, and he paused for a moment to watch. What was she doing, walking around the stall, patting walls?

"What's up?" he said at last.

She jumped, gasped and twirled around to face him. "It's you!" she said, clapping a hand to her chest as though to keep her heart in place.

He stared at her a second, but the sight of her drove every coherent thought from his head. She was wearing the white halter top with her jeans. Her golden skin glowed even in the subdued indoor light. After a quick look to make sure they were alone, he strode toward her.

"Yeah it's me," he said, advancing steadily. She backed up, almost tripping over herself. "What were you doing just now?"

"Nothing," she said quickly. He reached forward, grabbing her upper arms, pulling her toward him. "Like hell," he said.

"I just—"

But he didn't give her another chance to lie. Instead, he crushed his mouth against hers. After a second's hesitation, she wrapped her arms around his neck and kissed him back with the same longing and the same neediness he'd felt building in his own body. He lifted her from her feet and buried himself in her warm softness.

The kiss dissolved into another until she pressed her hands gently against his chest and he came up for air.

"Pete—"

"Shush," he said, his lips touching hers.

"Someone will see us. Put me down."

"I don't care. I can't stand not touching you."

She bit her lip and it seemed for a moment her eyes filled with tears, but in the next instant the tears were gone. The gentle Elle he treasured was gone. She was replaced by the other Elle, the one who always made him a little uneasy. She said, "I was just looking over this stall."

This Elle, to her credit, always knew how to grab his attention. He lowered her to her feet. "Why?"

"The water bucket is back," she said, pointing to the wall behind him.

Sure enough, the bucket was there, right where it belonged. He looked at the perfect bracket.

"The whole apparatus is new," Elle said. "I asked Tom where it came from. He didn't know. He's either stupid or crafty. I don't know which—"

"Stop," he said, advancing on her again. He pulled her close and added, "Elle, this could be very dangerous. Don't talk about this again."

"But I keep thinking about the way Jorge lurked around this stall."

He stared at her for a seconds, his mind racing. "What do you mean?"

She threw up a hand as though exasperated. "I'm not sure what I mean. It's just that the horse transports come and go, feed sacks come and go, this stall never has a horse in it, Tom is never around and knows very little about horses and won't answer any of my questions. Plus Jorge hung out here and now Jorge is dead. The water bucket—I think something is going on, that's all."

He stared into her eyes. "Elle, promise me you won't say a thing about this to anyone else."

"Why—"

"Damn it, just promise me. I hear what you're saying, trust me to look into it."

"I don't see how—"

"Please."

She narrowed her eyes. He resisted the urge to tie her up and tuck her someplace safe, like, say, Alaska.

She finally said, "Okay."

He wasn't sure if he believed her. Curiosity seemed to be her middle name. He said, "Suppose you're right? Suppose something fishy is going on down here. If it got Jorge killed, it could get you killed."

"Yes, okay, I got it."

"Meanwhile, Alazandro wants a party. He thinks if he pours enough tequila down his employees' throats they won't run away after payday. You get to organize it."

"Great. When does he want it?"

Pete glanced at his watch. "In about eleven hours."

The look on her face made him smile. "I'll go into town and get what you need," he said.

"I can send someone—"

"No, that's okay. I have a couple of other errands to run. And remember, no poking around."

He ducked into Meacham's office before leaving the stable.

ELLE SAT with her back to the swimming pool, still unable to bear looking at the beautiful fountain.

Considering the time limitations, she thought she'd done a pretty good job of getting the fiesta organized. Softly glowing paper lanterns dangled from ropes strung tree to tree, the band played music that seemed to lighten the humid air. People were well fed and half sober.

She'd spent much of the evening visiting with Steve, the copilot of Alazandro's personal jet. Part of her wanted to ask him for a ride home. He reminded her of a guy she'd dated in college though it was really just the name. This Steve was nearer to forty than twenty. His deep auburn hair reminded her of Mike back at Peg's stable.

"There's been a lot happening around here lately," he said as they watched people dance.

"Yeah. Rudy and Jorge—"

"Terrible thing, Rudy dying. Running into that pool, falling into the deep end. It's so awful."

She put her hand over his. "I hear he died quickly."

"Still. Makes you wonder, doesn't it?"

"What do you mean?" she prompted when his voice faded.

He leaned closer over the table. "A girl died here two months ago."

"Did you know Amber?"

"Was that her name? No, but I hear people talk. They say you're Mr. Alazandro's new girlfriend."

"Do they?"

"That's what I hear. You be careful."

Elle smiled. "Thanks for your concern, but it's not like that. I work for Mr. Alazandro, just like you do. How long have you been flying, Steve?"

"For Alazandro? Just a couple of months. Listen, if you ever want to catch a flight stateside, just let me know."

"And leave this paradise?"

"Paradise," he mused, shifting his beer bottle from one hand to the other. "It is beautiful here, isn't it?"

"Very."

Alazandro chose that moment to show up. Pete stood way off to the side leaving Alazandro by himself, unprotected, out in the open. If she had a gun and a confession and didn't care if she lived or died, she could put an end to all this right now.

Alazandro spoke with warmth and cunning, shaking hands, gripping shoulders, wincing only slightly when his own injured shoulder was clasped in a boozy embrace. He played the role of host perfectly, his relaxed demeanor as comforting as the tequila. He promised another bonus next month to those who stayed and shook his head sadly over the terrible misfortunes of the two dead men.

Elle turned to compare notes with Steve, but he'd wandered off to talk to the pilot. Instead, Pete was at her elbow. "Do you think it worked?" he asked.

"If nothing else happens around here, maybe."

His hand lingered on her arm, his touch enough to make her tremble. "Stay with me tonight," he whispered close to her ear. Their eyes met and she felt woozy with the desire his words inflamed.

"I can't. You know that," she whispered.

"Can't or won't?"

"It doesn't matter. The results are the same. I have to be smart."

"Is that what they're calling it now?" he said, his voice edgy. "Being smart?"

She shook her head. Movement behind Pete's shoulder revealed Alazandro zooming in on her, weaving his way through the people clearing the tables, the tall Asian man behind him. Willing herself to focus on Alazandro, she stood up and moved forward, grasping both his hands and complimenting his performance.

"It did go well," he bragged, rocking back on his heels. "Come on, Elle, we'll celebrate at my place."

"Can you wait a few moments?" she said, still avoiding Pete's gaze. "I need to make a quick trip down to the stables. There's another transport due tomorrow morning and I promised Tom Meacham I'd check everything over."

"And then you'll come back? We've had nothing but interruptions. No more."

"I'll come back."

She felt Pete stiffen beside her. "Where is Tom?" he said.

"He was here earlier, but he had a headache. I gather he lives in town."

"The bunkhouse isn't good enough for him," Alazandro said, a petulant note stealing into his voice. "Don't take long," he added. "Tonight's our night, *cariña.*"

Elle's heart raced as Alazandro kissed her hand. There were any number of lethal weapons in the stable. The awl used for punching holes in leather. The hoof knife, even the small knife used for cutting twine. *If the opportunity presented itself, she'd be ready.*

"I'll make sure she gets back to you safe and sound," Pete said, his voice devoid of emotion.

She was walking ahead of him when she sensed he'd stopped. She turned abruptly to find him staring past the clean-up crew, back toward the mosaic of the sun that hid the entrance to Alazandro's place.

"What's wrong?" she said.

"I just saw someone sneaking around back there. Stay here!" he snapped and, reaching inside his jacket, drew his gun, moving quickly between people, weapon held low.

"Like hell," Elle muttered and hurried after him.

She heard the muted sound of gunfire right as Pete disappeared behind the mosaic. By the time she lunged around the corner, Pete was shoving Alazandro inside his apartment. The big guard lay on the ground, a dark spot flowering on his pale shirt.

"Someone tried to shoot Alazandro," Pete snapped. "Help me get Shen Kuai inside."

The two of them dragged the injured man through the door where he sagged onto the floor. Elle fell to her knees, grabbed a sofa cushion and pressed it against Shen Kuai's chest. Alazandro was on the phone, hopefully calling for a doctor. Elle heard him bark, "Absolutely no sirens."

"Get Alazandro to lock the door after me," Pete said. And with that, he ran off into the night.

PETE SKIRTED THE BUILDING, hugging shadows. He'd lost time getting Alazandro to safety and helping Elle get Shen Kuai inside, but it couldn't be helped.

His main priority was keeping Alazandro alive until all his cronies showed up next week. If Alazandro died now, his buddies would scurry back into the woodwork.

He'd turned the corner in time to see a figure dressed head to toe in black with a ski mask over his face, struggling with Shen Kuai. The attacker had carried a pistol fitted with a silencer and that's probably what had saved both Alazandro and his bodyguard. The would-be assassin had to repeatedly fire close-up and personal to make those subsonic bullets do their deed—they didn't travel fast enough for a single hit to kill from a distance.

Shen Kuai, being as big as a mountain, had taken one shot. Alazandro's building had taken the rest.

Pete heard an engine turn over out near the stable. A moment later, headlights swept a paddock and the white horse standing inside it. The car passed under an overhead light. All Pete could tell was that it was an old blue sedan.

The same one as on the first night? Who knew?

He thought of calling the guard at the gate and telling him to detain the car. Even as he watched, other engines started, other headlights popped on as those employees who lived off the resort made their way home.

As he started back to Alazandro's place, he contemplated breaking his cover and telling Elle who he was. He was angry with her, he was disappointed in her, but he couldn't bear the thought of something bad happening to her.

He abandoned the idea almost immediately. Safer for her if she never knew any of this until it was over.

Another thought struck him. Alberto Montega and Ciro Ramos weren't guests tonight. They were both too well known at the gate to have snuck into the party unnoticed, which meant neither one of them had attempted to shoot Alazandro. If they'd hired a professional, they weren't getting their money's worth because Alazandro had now survived at least three clumsy attempts on his life.

AMAZINGLY, no word of what happened after the party spread through the resort. By the afternoon of the next day, Shen Kuai was on a plane bound for the States.

When Tom failed to show up for work the next morning, Elle was sure he was behind the latest murder attempt and maybe all the others, too. He was always absent when something awful happened. He didn't know much about horses or people. What if he'd been behind the payroll skimming and blamed it on Jorge? What if Jorge had found out?

Time was running out. Alazandro wasn't the kind of man to stay in one place long and his time here had been filled with nothing but trouble. Mexico was her best bet for exacting revenge without getting caught. Once he hit the States, it would all get harder. She was also living on her grandfather's money and that would go just so far.

She'd noticed the liver chestnut mare favoring her right front foot earlier, and was just dislodging a sharp stone with a hoof pick when a man's shadow fell over her. With a catch in her heart, she looked up to find Pete staring down at her.

"Alazandro wants you," he said.

She'd been curt with him that day and the night before. She couldn't afford to grow any more attached to him than she already had. She knew he cared for her, she knew he'd been tortured by past relationships, she didn't want to be the next blonde in his life to prove women were all a waste of time. She'd already allowed him close enough that in the end, her betrayal of Alazandro would hurt him.

He held the shotgun in one hand as they walked up to the resort. Elle just hoped he never had to use it on her.

ALAZANDRO SAT AT HIS TABLE, papers spread out around him.

As he finished working, Elle took in the obvious signs of his wealth. She tried to picture his world twenty years before. Into drugs, into gangs, up to no good. Obviously smart and glib, but on a fast track to nowhere.

He'd been at her house the day her family was found, the envelope and his descriptions of their deaths proved that. He'd been questioned by the police, evidence pointed to him, an arrest had been imminent, then evidence disappeared. He left the area, went south, put himself through college, became what he was today.

In essence, he'd built the world he lived in on the corpses of her family.

"I want to know how the progress on the beach property and the trail are going," he said abruptly.

"I sent a crew out yesterday to look at the trail," she said. "They went back today to continue their work. I have another crew due from Mexico City tomorrow. They're approaching the cove both by land and by boat with supplies they'll ferry onto the beach to work on the building."

"And how long will it take them?"

"A month. Hopefully."

"Too long."

"I was under the impression you wanted it ready for the resort opening—"

"Change of plans," he said. "I have an important meeting next week."

Confused, she muttered, "Hotel people?"

He stared at her a second before nodding. "Yeah, hotel people. I hoped to…entertain them here, at the resort, but Pete still hasn't nabbed the psycho who's trying to kill me." He slid Pete a frustrated glance before adding, "I've decided to take my associates on this trip you've been pushing. Better if we go somewhere neutral anyway. You've got less than forty-eight hours."

"That's impossible."

He raised his eyebrows.

She said, "It'll be…rustic."

"As long as it's private. We have business."

"I'll arrange generators for cooling. They'll make enough noise to cover—"

He waved off the details. "There'll be about ten of us. We'll have to take adequate security, plus they'll each bring someone of their own. Pete will see to that. Remember, when it comes to food and drink, these people are used to the best."

"Everything will have to be transported to the site."

"Whatever. No one here is to know about this event until we ride away Monday morning. Is that clear?"

"Of course, but we'll need grooms and feed—"

"Send all personnel a day early. Just don't tell them where they're going until you have to. Have things shipped directly. Keep this quiet. I want air transport out of there the next morning. I won't be coming back here."

Elle met his gaze. "Where are you going?"

"Don't you worry about that."

Heart in her throat, she blurted out, "But I have to know. I have to make plans—"

She stopped abruptly, noticing for the first time both men staring at her with puzzled expressions. What had she just said? The words were only twenty seconds old and already they were lost in the haze of panic. All she knew was that she didn't have Alazandro's resources, she couldn't chase him all over the world. And she was so close.

"What kind of plans?" Alazandro said, his voice deceptively soft. For the first time since meeting him, he sounded not only egotistical, sexist and elitist, but dangerous.

She blinked a couple of times and said, "Nothing."

He stared at her another moment before continuing. "After I'm gone, you'll come back here and keep things going until the new resort manager shows up to take over. You have a good way with people."

"How about that, Elle?" Pete murmured. "Just what you wanted. A promotion."

She cast him a wary look. But in her mind's eye, she saw only the steep cliff above the crescent beach and the jagged rocks below.

And her last chance.

PETE ROLLED THE RUBBER MAT to one side and revealed the trap door Tom Meacham had told him he'd found. He took another look around the stable. It was risky to be doing this, but the image of Tom laying in the dirt, a bullet hole through his forehead, had woken Pete in the middle of the night.

He opened the trap door with trepidation and, using a flashlight, descended a short ladder.

What he found was a large room with low overhead. No Tom, dead or alive. No stacks of feed bags as Tom had reported finding in the first cryptic message he'd delivered to Pete. The second message had reported he was going to investigate further during the party while everyone was preoccupied. From what Pete could gather, Tom hadn't been seen or heard from since then.

A thick layer of straw covered the dirt floor. A few saddle racks with saddles aboard were scattered about. Everything looked perfectly normal.

Which meant someone had emptied out the room after Tom visited it the first time. Pete had a sinking feeling he knew who and why. It wouldn't pay to get caught down here and he climbed out quickly, replacing everything as it had been and exiting the barn, his gaze darting every which way.

Unable to sleep, he put the finishing touches on the package he would leave at the gas station later that day. It included a bulletin on what Tom had found and the fact that it and Tom were now missing; the tape from the machine, rescued in a harrowing moment right as Alazandro climbed the stairs; information marked urgent concerning the new meeting time and location; a suggestion the DEA contact the Mexicans and arrange for a joint infiltration of the caterers and air transports Elle had hired.

And lastly, a request for a more in-depth background check on Elle Medina.

He'd always known she had a secret—last night was the first time he'd sensed her secret was in danger of crashing into his mission. He knew almost everything about her except for the years before her parents died. Her adopted father, the man she called the judge, had made sure those years were buried deep.

He had to find out what was going on. No matter how he felt about her, he couldn't allow her agenda to get in his way.

Chapter Twelve

Monday morning was a whirlwind of last-minute arrivals, departing horse transports and a million and one things to do.

Tom Meacham still hadn't shown up for work. Some of the men had stopped by his house in Las Brisas and reported his car gone, his house empty.

Elle felt uneasy about Tom, but she put that uneasiness aside. She had one job to do now and less than twenty-four hours in which to do it. She needed a confession and a means of exacting revenge in that order. Afterward?

There was no afterward. She might get Alazandro away for a tryst, but she wouldn't get away from Pete. She knew that. But hope dies eternal and, just in case, she stuffed her passport in her saddlebag.

As she saddled her horse, she wondered why Pete didn't suspect Tom. It had to be because he knew Tom *wasn't* guilty because he knew who *was* guilty. On the other hand, maybe she didn't know Pete as well as she thought she did.

As she cinched the saddle, she spied Pete standing by the completed mosaic in front of the resort's main doors. He wore a pair of wraparound sunglasses she'd never seen before, a hi-tech looking pair that, along with his stance—hands held behind the back, legs slightly apart—made him look official. All that was missing was a black suit, though he wore his jeans, white shirt and buckskin vest with his usual aplomb.

She knew he'd sent ahead a team of security people to the beach location just as she'd sent ahead feed and grooms for the horses and arranged for caterers. Everyone who had left the ranch had left with destination unknown until they'd ridden past Las Brisas, at which time they'd been told. Seaplanes would land in the cove come morning to whisk everyone back to the airport and their own rides home. She marveled over the extravagant outlay of money for a mere twelve-hour meeting with a bunch of hotel people.

She rode at the head of the party, Pete rode at the rear. There were twenty-three men between them, all dressed like dandies, but all good riders; her nightmare that some hotel tycoon would go plunging off the hillside seemed unfounded. They bypassed Las Brisas.

When Elle had suggested this scenario to Alazandro, she'd envisioned a jolly ride full of laughing and eager anticipation. Men and women, romance in the air. She hadn't anticipated the stony silence and every-man-to-himself aura of this group.

Alazandro rode directly behind Elle. As the trail began the long decline to the beach below, she pulled to a stop and turned around in her saddle. Addressing the men in Spanish, she said, "I'll go down first and make sure the trail is good. There's been a lot of traffic on it the last day or two but I haven't had a chance to check it out personally."

"I'll go with you," Alazandro said. He, in turn, faced the rest of the group and added, "Everyone wait here."

Elle's heart kicked into overdrive. She looked along the lines of horses and men until she saw Pete, trapped at the back.

She would be alone with Alazandro on the trail.

PETE WATCHED ELLE AND ALAZANDRO ride off. He asked the man in front of him what was going on, not because he didn't know, he'd heard all right, but because he was the only one of the men Pete had failed to get a decent picture of yet.

Rueben Garcia of Tijuana turned around and stared right through Pete. Pete, still wearing his new spy sunglasses, hit the remote in his pocket and snapped the man's stony-faced image.

Excusing himself, he rode along the verge at the edge of the path until he reached the front and took off after Elle and Alazandro, calling to the others to wait.

He caught up with them at the wide spot where the trail looked over the rocky shore. Elle had gotten off her horse, Alazandro was still on his. Alazandro's horse skittered near the edge. Elle put a hand on its rump, and then immediately grabbed the bridle with her other hand and pulled the animal back from the precipice.

"Hey," Pete said as she turned to face him. "That was a close call."

She looked pale and uneasy as she quickly looked away without commenting. A knife twisted in his heart. He'd lost her and he wasn't even sure why.

FOR ELLE, riding at last onto the beach was anticlimatic.

She'd blown her chance. All she'd had to do was slap the skittish animal's rump and the beautiful roan gelding would have carried Alazandro to the bottom of the cliff and certain death.

Without a confession.

It wasn't just the lack of a confession that had stopped her, though. In the moment she'd considered sacrificing that prerequisite, she'd found she couldn't sacrifice the innocent horse. Man, she was so screwed up she'd never be normal again.

But if her compassion for the horse hadn't stayed her hand, Pete would have seen the whole thing.

The beach and its modest building had been transformed almost overnight. The building itself had been swept clean in preparation for the coming meeting. Windows were covered, doors had been installed. A generator worked overtime fueling an air conditioner.

The caterers had set up a huge white tent to the right of the building to use for food prep. As she approached, Elle could see all the flaps had been tied up to allow what breeze there was to pass through. Waiters carrying trays greeted Alazandro and his guests with cold drinks and hors d'oeuvres. Seating had been arranged and the men seemed to relax as they formed informal groups. Back by the palm trees, smaller white tents were pinned with names as stable hands delivered the guests' belongings to what would serve as their nighttime lodging. The armed guards stood around looking important.

For Elle, the extravagant beauty of it all made everything just hurt more. From where she stood at the edge of the big tent, she could see the shadowed end of the beach where she and Pete had stripped each other bare in more ways than one and fallen into each other's arms. She closed her eyes against the bittersweet memories.

After a rest, three of the stable hands took some of the

horses back to the resort. Elle and the other stable hands would take the remainder of them back the next day. And Alazandro would go flying off to safety.

Unless she found the courage and the opportunity to do what had to be done.

And there was an additional puzzle to figure out. Why did all these hotel tycoons travel with armed guards? Had they all received death threats? Was there some unlikely plot to rid the world of Mexican entrepreneurs?

Or was there more going on here than she'd allowed herself to consider before? And if so, did Pete know about it? Was Pete part of it?

A wave of unease washed through her stomach. It was entirely possible she wasn't the only one on this beach with secrets.

NIGHT CAME, and with it, the beach camp achieved a level of exotic romanticism totally wasted on the group at hand. Though prepared food and expensive wine were served at round tables that had been set up near the water, each on its own woven mat, flanked by its own flaming torches, the guests ate in a kind of somber wariness. Maybe it was the off note provided by the armed men patrolling the beach and head of the trail, flashlights making wide arcs in the pristine darkness. At any rate, though it looked right to Elle, it didn't feel right.

As the night wore on, the tables were moved from under the stars to inside the building. One by one, the men disappeared inside, the guards taking up posts all around the perimeter.

Elle declined an invitation to stretch out her sleeping bag inside the catering tent for the night. Instead, she wandered close to the bluff and found a dark shadow where she could lurk without being noticed. Sooner or later, Alazandro would leave the building for his own tent. And she'd be ready.

She just about jumped out of her skin when a hand closed over her mouth at the same time an arm snaked around her waist.

"Keep quiet," Pete said, turning her to face him. He removed his hands. "Come here."

She followed him several feet away, her heart still pounding. Or pounding anew. It was the first time he'd touched her in days and there was no denying the icy hot chills he created. When he stopped abruptly, she bumped into him. Her body seemed to go into stimulation overload.

"What the hell are you doing?" he said, his voice low but quivering with anger. A stray shaft of light glinted off the barrel of the gun as he shoved it back in his shoulder holster.

"What I do is none of your—"

"Do you realize how many men are standing around here anxious to shoot first and ask questions later?"

"So why aren't you over with the rest of them?"

He was silent for a second before saying, "I can see everything fine from over there."

"So tell me the truth," she said bluntly. "What the hell is going on?"

"I don't—"

"Give me a break. Since when do a bunch of wealthy tycoons meet on a remote beach with enough firepower to take over a third-world country?"

"I don't—"

"It's Alazandro, isn't it? He's not just into building

resorts and cheating nice ladies out of their land. He's into something worse, isn't he?"

Silence.

She thought for a second. The weird going-ons at the stable popped into her mind. "Drugs?" More silence. "So you're the kind of man who works for a drug dealer?"

He swore softly. "Elle—"

"I can't believe it," she whispered. Tears stung the back of her nose.

"What do you care what I am?" he growled. "You've made it very clear you don't give a damn."

"How can you be so stupid?" she hissed.

"You've been avoiding me like the plague."

"You're a damn thug. You're bodyguard to a man who peddles poison. After that sob story about your old girl-friend's drug habit—"

"Now who's being stupid?"

She could barely make out his features. Her heart beat so fast it felt ready to erupt from her chest like a rocket ship. And in that instant, she finally got a glimpse of what was really going on.

"You're more than just his bodyguard, aren't you?" she whispered.

"I can't—"

"It all makes sense now. That's why you've allowed all these terrible things to happen without getting involved."

"Elle, please, stop. Lower your voice."

"I knew the only reason you wouldn't suspect Tom Meacham is if you were guilty or you knew he wasn't," she whispered. "You're some kind of secret agent."

"Please. I work undercover for the DEA."

"Same thing. Tom is an agent, too, isn't he? That's how you know he didn't kill Jorge."

After an exceptionally long pause, Pete sighed deeply. "I just found out Jorge was with Mexican drug enforcement," he said haltingly. "He and Tom were working on the same case but they didn't know it."

"Something to do with the stable."

"Drugs coming through the stable."

"Inside the feed sacks brought north in all those horse transports?" His head dipped in the briefest of nods. "I knew something was going on," she added.

"I think they use the horse transports to throw off the Mexican police. The last transport is being tailed right now."

"Is Alazandro's dude ranch buddy really some kind of drug peddler?"

"Yes. That's what this meeting is all about. Alazandro has gathered together the head of several cartels. They're talking expansion by combining forces."

"I knew they weren't hotel people."

"No. And they're dangerous, remember that. My contact says Jorge reported Alazandro's men in the stable were growing suspicious. And that was the day you went riding with him. By that night he was dead."

"And those charges that he was skimming pay?"

"I think Alazandro had inside information about Jorge. I think he tried to discredit him with that skimming charge, maybe hoping one of the men would kill him and save Alazandro the trouble."

"Why was his body in the pool when they must have drowned him in that damn water bucket?"

"You can't blame an accidental drowning on a water bucket mounted several feet off the floor. I'm guessing that right after they dumped Jorge in the pool, they saw you being carried off and decided it would look better to toss Jorge over the bluff. With any luck, his death and your disappearance wouldn't be connected. Alazandro might own the local police, but a missing or dead American citizen is another matter. Especially after Amber Linn's death a couple of months ago."

"Which brings us to Tom."

"No one has heard from him for days. I know he found a storage unit. He reported it was full of feed sacks. He suspected they all contained methamphetamines. He went back to check during the party. Someone must have seen him searching, grown suspicious and decided to cut their losses. By the time I looked, they'd cleaned the place out. This kind of thing couldn't be going on without several of the stable hands knowing about it. One or two of them is probably sleeping over there by the horses. And I'd bet a bundle at least one of them is a murderer."

"But why would Alazandro kill Rudy?"

"Rudy's death may have been an accident or it may be linked to the other attempts on Alazandro and his bodyguards and you, too, for that matter. I thought Montega and Ciro were involved but it seems so hit and miss for supposed professionals."

He touched her arm and, as one, they walked quickly a few feet farther away.

"There's something else you need to know," he said, lowering his voice even more.

"I have to tell you something, too."

He touched her face and her insides melted. It was literally hard to stand and yet he did no more than draw three fingertips across her cheek. He lowered his mouth until his lips were a mere inch from hers and whispered, "You first."

What she wanted to do was tell him how he made her

feel. She wanted him to know that no matter what happened in the future, no matter what she did and what he thought about it, he'd know her feelings for him were genuine. Yet how could she justify saying anything that would give him hope? Tears pooled in her eyes and ran down her cheeks, dripping across her lips.

Gripping his arms and rising on her tiptoes, she closed the distance between them. Her lips touched his with a jolt. He pulled her against him and kissed her with so much pent-up longing it took her breath away. His heart was right there for her to take, to break, but she couldn't do it, not like this. It wasn't fair and she sought to push him away. But it was as though her bones had dissolved and her effort translated into nothing more than surrender.

The next thing she knew, he'd picked her up. She didn't want to think. She couldn't imagine where he was taking her. When the ocean became louder and spray stung her skin, she clung to him. He rounded the rocky point to emerge on a smaller beach. He lowered her to the sand and stared down at her from his knees and she opened her arms, opened her heart, knowing she shouldn't, unable to resist.

The world became only him. His warm, wet mouth, the heat of his body, his hands sliding under her clothes, hers sliding across his bare flesh, both of them exploring, caressing, starting deep, hot fires until once again, very quietly but with overwhelming power, he entered her. She willed her body to declare what her voice could not.

She loved him. For better or worse. For now, forever.

UNWILLING TO BE TRAPPED by the rising tide, Pete led Elle back around the rocks to his sleeping bag which he'd set out in a dark hollow by the bluff. They leaned back against the rock, her silky hair spilling over his shoulder. He was keyed up, his mission almost in the bag. Plus, bonus, he was in love with Elle and even if she didn't love him, he knew she had feelings for him.

Life looked pretty damn good. Now all he had to do was keep her alive. "I have to tell you something," he whispered, hoping she was awake.

She stirred against him and he felt her breasts press against his side as she turned. Willing himself to concentrate on things other than making love to her again, he said, "Things are going to happen tomorrow morning."

"What do you mean?" she murmured.

"The caterers are all Mexican agents, the pilots flying in tomorrow are our guys. I have a contact in the caterers, in fact, he's standing guard right now. He's the one who told me about Jorge. When this all starts coming down tomorrow, I want you to stay out of the way until it's over."

Her voice sound faraway as she said, "What about Alazandro?"

"He'll be extradited to the U.S. where he'll face drug and racketeering charges among other things. We couldn't get things together fast enough to do it tonight."

She'd grown stiff in his arms. For one terrible moment he wondered if she was disappointed Alazandro was going down. But he let that thought go. He still didn't know what she was up to, but he knew it wasn't a job promotion. "It's time you were straight with me," he said.

It took her forever to answer. She finally said, "Not tonight. I have to think. I have to…think."

"Tomorrow," he said, kissing her forehead.

"Yes," she murmured, her voice so soft he had to strain to hear it. "Let's try to get some sleep."

He didn't protest but he knew sleep was not on his agenda for the night. He was too hyped, his mind raced, he kept going over the details. The planes would land and launch inflatable rafts, everything would appear normal to the men on the beach. It would be up to him and the Mexican agents posing as caterers to disarm the guards. He reviewed the plans in his mind as the moon rose in the sky and Elle dozed at his side. He found his eyes drifting shut...

He awoke with a start. It was still dark.

Elle was gone.

His hand went immediately to his holster—his gun was gone, too.

ELLE STOPPED HER HORSE at the turn out on the trail. Alazandro pulled his horse up beside hers. The early morning sky was clear and bright.

Voice bordering on incredulous, he said, "Here?"

"I've been having fantasies about this very place," she said. Nerves made her breathless. He misread nerves as excitement and immediately got off the gelding.

She got off her horse, too, and led both animals away from the edge of the cliff where she tied their reins through the loop of an unearthed root.

Alazandro stood with hands at his waist, open space behind him. She'd found him in his tent and seduced him to within an inch of his wildest hopes, promising culmination if he came with her, right then, no questions asked. He'd followed like a lamb to slaughter, ordering guards out of his way, so caught up in lust he hadn't asked questions.

She'd had to move fast. If she waited until daylight, he'd be arrested with everyone else, moved into the criminal justice system from which her family had never received any justice. If she waited, he'd be gone, a twenty-year-old triple murder small potatoes compared to what he'd done lately.

She'd had to put Pete out of her mind as she kissed Alazandro and allowed him to kiss her. She'd become another person. And now they were high on the bluff and the end was finally drawing near.

"Here on this ledge, in the dirt, *cariña*?" he said. "*This* is what turns you on?" He laughed gustily. "And all the time I've been plying you with silk sheets and champagne."

She reached behind her back, drew Pete's gun, and leveled it at Alazandro's head. "I'm just a simple country girl," she said.

His smile faded as his eyes narrowed. "This is part of the fantasy?" he demanded.

"Kind of."

"I don't—"

"I want you to say it," she told him.

"You want me to say what?" His voice had grown wary.

Too little, too late.

"I want you to confess to murdering my family," she said.

"Your family? What are you talking about—"

"The Seattle cop. His name was Kirk Foster. My mother, Eileen. My baby brother, Sammy. I know you shot them to death. Now I want to hear you tell me."

As she talked, she dug trenches in the earth with the heel of her boot. With any luck at all, she could sell the story of a secret rendezvous gone bad, Alazandro falling to his death. She wouldn't think of what the story would do to Pete. She'd send Alazandro's horse on up the trail, riderless, throw his saddle down after him. No one would remember what horse he rode, no one would care.

Maybe she could get away. If not, so be it.

She kicked a couple of big rocks over the edge, uprooting a few plants. Alazandro grew pale as a ghost as they all careened off the steep rocky crag on their journey to the sea far below.

They both looked up as a half dozen seaplanes approached from the south. The rising sun glistened off their wings.

"Tell me," she said.

"I can't tell you what didn't happen," he said, his gaze darting between the gun and the edge dangerously close to his heels. He licked his lips.

"Don't lie," she cautioned.

"I didn't know the cop—"

"You gave him an envelope."

His gaze shifted as if he apparently tried to remember what he'd told her. He finally said, "Okay, so I kind of knew him." She crowded him with the gun held tight to her body. He backed up. Dirt spilled over the edge and he scrambled for safer ground but she stood in the way of his breaking free. She had to hurry. He was already looking around, trying to find a way to overpower her. She didn't want to shoot him, she didn't want his body found with a bullet hole—

"What are you doing?" he screamed.

The seaplanes would drown out any noise he made, but time was limited. "Tell me!" she demanded, kicking dirt at his legs, her emotions getting the better of her.

"What? That I killed them?" He glanced at the eroding earth around his feet and then back at her. "Okay, okay, I killed them. I killed them all."

It was like a bolt slammed into place in her heart. "I knew it," she said. "You came to our house. You brought the envelope—"

"I brought a tape inside an envelope. The cop was paying me to rat on my friends. He promised me I could walk—"

"He reneged on his promise of amnesty for you, didn't he? That's why you murdered them."

"Yes. Now get me away from this edge—"

"Where's Tom Meacham?"

"Meacham. I don't—"

She cocked the gun. "Yes you do. Where is he?"

He glanced behind then back at her, his expression desperate. "Buried in the store room under one of the stalls, okay?" he yelled.

"Why?"

"Why? He found our stash, that's why. Back off—"

"Your stash of meth, headed north to Tijuana and then the United States?"

"Yes, yes. So what? Junk for losers, who cares?"

"You're going to jump off this mountain," she said softly. "For my family, for Jorge, for Rudy and for Tom."

His eyes widened at the names of the others but it was quickly chased away by a new wave of fear. "But I confessed—"

"Yes. And now you're going to pay. Think of me as their avenging angel, Víctor. It's over."

She waved the gun and he took a halting step back toward oblivion….

"ONE'S MISSING," an American agent said. He handed Pete a small envelope and added, "Any idea where Alazandro went?"

"No." Alazandro's absence was the only sour note in an otherwise pretty smooth operation. Gunfire had been limited to one death, an overzealous guard. Three other men sustained injuries. It was thought Alazandro had escaped. Pete was worried sick that it was more than that because he knew Elle was gone, too, a fact everyone else seemed to have missed.

He opened the envelope as the other agent answered a call on his cell phone. Out in the cove, the first seaplane took off with the injured men and the first of the drug czars on his way to jail. The agent covered the phone with his hand. Gesturing at the envelope, he said, "I was told you requested that."

"Any word on Tom Meacham?"

The agent shook his head. "Not yet." He went back to his phone call as Pete slipped the papers from the envelope.

"There's a girl missing, too," the agent said as he pocketed his phone.

Pete barely heard him. He was reading about Elle's early life and what he read twisted his gut into a knot. He looked up at the agent. "What did you say?"

"They say there was a woman here but she's gone."

"Alazandro must have taken her," Pete said.

The agent looked perplexed. "She's with Alazandro? Is she part of his organization—"

"No," Pete said. "We've got to find her, though. Listen, I took her around the point last night. Get someone to see if she went that way or if Alazandro did."

"Where are you going?" the agent asked as Pete took off toward the palm trees.

He didn't stop to answer.

It was her family Alazandro had been accused of murdering. How stupid could he be, how dense, how caught up in his own emotions and feelings that he hadn't used his brain, that he hadn't seen what she was doing—

All the questions, all the time bringing the conversation back to the dead cop. *Her father!*

As Pete saddled a horse, the past few days came flooding back into his head. She'd been hunting Alazandro right from the start, that's why she went hot and cold with the man, why she flirted with him even as her expression grew cold and remote.

She was after Alazandro. Pete had a sneaking suspicion where she might have taken him.

Unless he had this all mixed up and it was Alazandro who had taken her....

Chapter Thirteen

Pete got off his horse and stood at the wide spot high on the cliff face, his heart sinking as he took in the signs of a struggle. The deep gouges in the earth led right to the edge. He knew it was too far down to make out anything, but he looked anyway.

Nothing he could see. But something had happened here. One or the other, maybe both, had fallen to their death.

He took off up the path, urging the horse forward, breaking into a gallop when the trail finally opened up onto the plateau. He could think of no place the victor would go except back to the resort.

Why did he keep falling for crazy blondes? What was wrong with him that he gave his heart to women too broken to give love in return? Last night he'd thought they had a chance. Had she been using him to pass the time?

No. He couldn't afford to whitewash her intentions, but he didn't have to paint her evil, either. The truth was, he doubted her ability to kill Alazandro. Surely she'd had many opportunities before this. There was a huge chasm between planning a death and committing a murder, between evil intent and action. If she hadn't been able to kill Alazandro before this, then it was very likely she'd been the one to tumble off that cliff.

His heart rose in his throat and for a second, he almost turned around and rode back to the beach. No, he wouldn't allow himself to get trapped down there in that mess....

Trapped.

As he rode past the trail veering off to Las Brisas a new thought struck him. If Alazandro was still alive, he wouldn't allow himself to become trapped at the resort. Nor would Elle. They'd want to escape—

The airport. They'd go to the airport.

It took another twenty minutes of riding before he saw the big aluminum hangars, another ten minutes until the trail paralleled the tarmac.

The place was closed up this early in the morning, but he saw two horses tied up in the shade cast by the office building. Alazandro's small private jet sat off to one side, awaiting passengers. There wasn't a soul around.

The glass pane in the door was broken, the door stood ajar. Pete took his shotgun from the back of the saddle. As he plotted how to enter, Elle's voice called out. "In here. It's okay."

Dreading what he might find, he kicked the door open.

Elle sat on the desk. She'd taped Alazandro to a chair and held Pete's gun on him. She'd also stuffed a rag in his mouth. She glanced over her shoulder at Pete, grinned and said, "What took you so long?"

Alazandro made gurgling noises. Pete thought he saw a flash of hope in the older man's eyes. Of course, he thought Pete worked for him.

Ignoring Alazandro, Pete reached Elle in one step, and heedless of his gun, gathered her in a one-armed hug that smashed her against his chest. He kissed the top of her head. "I know about your family," he said. "I thought—"

"You thought I wanted to kill Alazandro," she said as he released her.

"Yes. My God, I thought you were out after revenge."

"You were absolutely right," she said. "But in the end, I couldn't kill him."

"He's not worth ruining your life for," Pete said.

"That wasn't it, though. I looked at him standing there and I saw the picture of his kids in my head. He's got a son, you know that? If I kill Alazandro, then the kid is going to have to come kill me. I guess I finally realized that revenge doesn't have an end, it just goes on and on. Besides, I discovered I'm not a killer."

"I know that."

"But he is. Not only did he kill my family, but you were right, he had someone kill Jorge. And Tom Meacham. His body is buried in that underground storeroom, the one I told you about. I as good as killed him—"

"That's the not way it works," Pete said, brushing away her tears. "You didn't kill anybody. Remember that." He held her against him as he flipped open his cell phone and called for a plane.

ELLE AND PETE WATCHED as the plane rolled to a stop. "I'll be right back. Don't take your eyes or the gun off him." He jogged off toward the plane while from a safe distance, Elle held a gun on Alazandro who, though untaped, was now hobbled and handcuffed. He regarded her with hooded eyes and a curled lip.

"Listen to me," he said.

She wished they'd left the gag in place. "No."

"I've killed three people with my own hands."

Her saddlebag lay by her feet. Maybe there was something in there she could stuff into his mouth. She refused to meet his eyes and prayed Pete would return before she had to listen to Alazandro brag.

"One was a boy who tried to knife me," he said. "We were both thirteen. He was bigger. I was stronger."

She glared at him for a moment as the import of his words sank into her head. "Who were the other two?"

"Does it matter? The point is, I did not kill your family. I had no reason to kill them. I was not at your house that day. I met your father the day before and gave him that envelope. I met him in a damn alley. I would not shoot a sleeping woman and an infant."

"You described how you killed them."

He shrugged. "I repeated what the cops told me, what I read in the paper. I was trying to impress you."

"You'll say anything to save your—"

His laughter interrupted her. "Why would I bother, Ms. Medina? Look at me. I'm not going anywhere. But I didn't kill your family. My alibi was the truth."

"There was evidence—"

"Ah, the evidence. Funny how it all just went away. How could I, a twenty-five-year-old drug pusher, infiltrate the police department and destroy or steal evidence? Think about it."

Pete was standing near the plane, talking to other agents. As he looked back at her, the sun illuminated his smile. He started back toward her, his body moving in that lanky, easygoing gait that set her skin on fire, a grin of satisfaction on his handsome, tanned face. In a flash, she saw what his son would look like someday. *Her son, too. If...*

He'd gone to make arrangements for them to leave on the plane with Alazandro. Fly to safety. Fly to the future.

"Think," Alazandro said.

Elle didn't have to think. She looked back at Alazandro. "Oh, please, no—"

At that moment, shots erupted from the direction of the hangar. Alazandro fell to his knees, then onto his face. Elle watched, horrified as Pete lifted his shotgun and returned fire.

The gunman collapsed, his deep auburn hair all that Elle could see.

Additional agents ran from the direction of the plane as a blue sedan erupted from behind the hangar and raced onto the tarmac. Elle saw the driver's face for an instant before he turned the car abruptly and took off on the road to Las Brisas.

While half the agents approached the fallen gunman, two more jumped into a different car and sped after the sedan. Pete perched on his heels, his fingers at Alazandro's throat. "He's been hit bad," he said, gently rolling Alazandro onto his back. He took off his vest and bunched it over the older man's stomach wound. Alazandro's eyelids flickered.

Elle knelt beside Pete. "The gunman," she said urgently. "It's Steve. It's Alazandro's copilot."

"I know."

"What's going on?"

"I'm not sure, but that blue sedan was missing a driver's side mirror."

"The driver was someone from the stable. I don't know his name but I recognize his face."

"Our assailants. Alazandro's assassins."

One of the other agents jogged up behind Pete. "What do you want to do about the plane?"

Pete glanced up at Elle, then over his shoulder at the

agent. "Escort Ms. Medina onto the plane and tell the pilot to get her out of here."

Elle watched as Alazandro's life seemed to ebb away. She said, "I can't—"

"Please, honey," Pete said softly, staring at her with his incredible blue eyes, both his hands pressing his vest against the wounds that leaked Alazandro's life away. "I'll catch up with you later today or tomorrow. I want you long gone before the Mexican police impound us all. I'll figure out the red tape later."

She slipped the gun into her saddlebag and nodded woodenly as the agent helped her stand. She walked away without feeling the tarmac beneath her feet, without feeling the blazing sun overhead—without feeling anything.

ALAZANDRO LICKED HIS LIPS and groaned.

"Stay still," Pete said. It was futile to try to stop the bleeding but he tried anyway. He knew in his heart they were waiting for an ambulance that wouldn't arrive in time.

Alazandro spoke a few words and Pete leaned closer.

Alazandro whispered, "She left...didn't she?"

Pete nodded. "She'll soon be far away."

A smile twitched Alazandro's lips. Pete felt a stab of uneasiness.

"You think you're going to get...happy...happy ever after. You think you can...ruin me...and...and walk away."

"What are you talking about?" Pete said, worried now Alazandro would die before he could explain. A siren's piercing wail announced its arrival at the airfield. Pete's hands clenched.

"She knows…" Alazandro whispered.

Pete leaned closer still. "She knows what?"

"She'll come…apart," Alazandro said with the ghost of a smile. "She won't…stop this time. So much harder when it's someone…someone you trust. She'll kill him."

"Kill who? What the hell are you talking about?

"The truth. Not…not me. Her father's partner…"

As the siren pulled up beside them, Alazandro's eyes went blank.

Pete stared at the dead man as the words sunk in. *Her father's partner.* The judge.

The bastard told Elle her adopted father killed her family. No wonder she'd looked stunned. No wonder she'd acted like she was in some kind of trance.

Was it true?

He had to stop her before she did something she'd regret forever. He swore under his breath as he realized his hope of her being a whole woman who could love and cherish him as he did her was just a fantasy. She'd been too damaged. His days of trying to rebuild a woman from the ground up were over.

He stared down at Alazandro and wished with all his heart this evil man had taken this last secret to his grave. It didn't matter. He had to get to Elle quickly….

Maybe he couldn't save her for himself, maybe there would never be a "them." But maybe he could save her for herself. That would have to be enough….

ELLE HAD CALLED FROM THE AIRPORT. She knew he was home.

She'd changed planes in hopes of avoiding interference from Pete. Just in case he knew. Just in case he suspected.

She'd entered the country driving a rental car. Customs had taken forever. She was sick at heart.

How could he have done this? Was it possible Alazandro had lied?

She'd seen the truth in his eyes.

She walked into the ranch house in which she'd spent most her childhood. All a lie. The place smelled of cigarette smoke. He'd promised her he'd quit. Was that a lie, too?

"That you, Elle?" he called. "I'm in the basement. Come on down."

The basement. Of course, it had to be the basement. She detoured to his gun case. She knew where he hid the key. She took a Glock from the case.

As she descended the stairs, she half expected to run into her father's rotting corpse climbing the stairs to greet her. She steeled herself against the images that ran through her mind as she held the gun out of sight behind her thigh.

But there was no corpse on the stairs, and none lying on the floor. That was all the past. Just the judge, sitting in his favorite recliner, smiling at her.

He was a big man with a ring of gray-white hair. He looked younger than his sixty-three years, though he'd put on weight lately, joking that his judicial robes covered the worst of it. He was dressed in a denim shirt and blue jeans. He looked in control—he always did.

He stood when he saw her.

"I got a call awhile ago from a man named Pete," he said. "He told me you were on your way. He also told me you wanted to hurt me."

"And what did you say?"

"I said you wouldn't hurt me, no matter what."

He was unarmed, relying as usual on his size and presence to intimidate people. Elle raised the gun and said, "You should have listened to him."

"Put that down, Elle. You don't need a gun."

"You shot at Alazandro," Elle said. "In Tahoe. You hit him in the arm."

"Yes."

"Peg took a shot, too."

The judge shook his head. "No, she didn't."

"I saw her with a gun—"

"She told me what happened. She said she went up in that damn loft to shoot herself. Thought it was the only way out of her troubles, but she changed her mind." He looked Elle straight in the eye and added, "I didn't shoot at you. There was another gunman—"

"I know. He got Alazandro this morning."

The judge nodded. "But that's not why you're here."

"You tried to kill Alazandro because you were worried he'd tell me the truth."

"No," he said, and then with a sigh that seemed to deflate him by half, murmured, "Yes."

Yes. The word echoed in Elle's brain. Despite their differences, this man had been a father to her. How could he have killed her family? Her stomach turned over.

"My plan was to kill Alazandro that morning," the judge added. "But I couldn't do it, so I winged him, hoping you'd get left behind. Then all hell broke loose and the next thing I knew, you were in the car and the car was flying out of there."

"You shot my mother and brother and father and brought me here," Elle said, her voice robotic. "You wouldn't even let my grandfather call me Janey, I had to be Elle. You buried my past and tried to blame an innocent man—"

He stopped her with one hand held up and for the first time in her life, she saw hesitancy in his eyes. He sagged back in the chair. It seemed he'd aged a decade in ten seconds.

"You want the truth," he said.

"I think I deserve that much."

"I've tried your whole life to protect you from it." He stared at the gun, blinked several times and said, "Sit down. You're going to need to sit down."

"I don't want to sit down," she insisted.

Sighing, he shook his head at her stubbornness. It was such a familiar gesture it made Elle's throat close.

"It started when your mother asked your father for a divorce."

"I don't—"

"Just listen to me. When Eileen told Kirk she wanted a divorce, he went ballistic. He left the house in a rage. She left a message on my private line, the one my wife never answered. I had a couple of days off and had gone hunting to get away, to think. I wasn't there for your mother. Or for your dad."

"Why would she want a divorce? She'd just had his baby—"

"Not his baby," he said, his voice cracking. "She had another man's baby and she wanted a divorce."

"She told him Sammy wasn't his?"

He nodded. "When he didn't come home that night, she went to bed in the spare room up in the attic. She didn't want to use their bedroom. He came back very early in the morning and found her asleep. He was out of his mind by this time, that's the only explanation. He shot her. It wasn't until he looked to make sure she was dead that he realized she'd taken the baby to bed with her and his bullet had killed little Sammy, too."

Elle's tears came in a steady stream as she said, "But he—"

"Elle, I don't think he really knew what he was doing when he killed your mother. He was so hurt. Not just with her cheating, but to find out his son wasn't his son. She told him she was leaving and taking you with her. It was just more than he could bear. But he didn't mean to hurt Sammy and when he discovered that baby dead in his mother's arms it was just the final straw. He went down to the basement and shot himself. He fell on the gun.

"He was so out of his mind by then that he never stopped to think what would happen when his little girl woke up and went searching for her family. Her mommy's bed and her brother's crib would be empty. All she'd find, if she didn't think to go up in the attic, would be her daddy in the basement. Thank God, Elle, you didn't go up in the attic. Your nightmares were bad enough without that—

"As it was, you were alone there with them in that house for well over twenty-four hours."

"You came that day," Elle murmured.

"Yes. I got home and heard your mother's message. I couldn't get through to your house. I found out later your father had cut the phone line. I raced over. Your birthday was the next day and there was a box on your front porch from your grandpa. I pounded on the door until you answered. I was so relieved to see you until you told me your daddy wouldn't wake up…"

His voice trailed off. His eyes seemed to be staring back inside his head.

Elle, choking on her own tears said, "How do you know all this? There wasn't a note."

He focused back on her. "There was a note. It was in his pocket. When I saw what had happened, I took you to the neighbor's house. I saw the envelope and tape from Alazandro lying on the floor beside your father as though he'd dropped it and it gave me the idea to blame everything on Alazandro. He deserved a murder rap, we all knew he'd killed at least one kid several years earlier. Your dad and I had been trying to nail his miserable hide for years. Why not let him go down for this? So I destroyed the suicide note and took the gun out of the house and re-arranged whatever needed rearranging. I knew your father had met with Alazandro the day before, I knew where the tape and envelope came from. It was my case and I just directed things the way I wanted."

"But why?"

He swallowed without speaking, without blinking until he finally mumbled, "Sammy was my baby. Your mother and I were going to run away together. I started it all, I had an affair with my partner's wife. I—I loved her. I was to blame, I couldn't let you know what your father had done. You were innocent like Sammy. I couldn't save him, but damn it, I could save you. And that's what I tried to do."

"What about the missing evidence?" Pete said.

Neither Elle or the judge had heard him enter the house or descend the stairs and as one, they turned to face him. Elle would have given a million dollars for the right to race to his arms, but she'd abandoned that right when she'd come here with the intent to kill.

Had that been her intent?

"I couldn't go through with my plan," the judge said. "In

the end, Alazandro hadn't committed the murder and I couldn't go through with it. Since everyone thought he did it, I'd achieved what I wanted. I called that good and got rid of everything I could. I packed Elle up and moved away. Went back to college, became a lawyer then a judge...and the rest...well, you know the rest, Elle. Janey."

A reel of that awful day as it must have appeared to him ran through her mind. The woman he loved and his only child, dead. His friend and partner, dead. His partner's five-year-old daughter alone in the world, trapped in a house of horrors. So, he'd done what he could to protect her.

He stood, a big man, slightly bowed, the cause of all the evil that had spilled into Elle's life.

Or was he?

People made mistakes. Her father's solution had been to murder, just as she'd thought she must do. But he'd been wrong...and so had she. Revenge was a circle....

She looked down at the Glock, still grasped in her hand.

Pete appeared in front of her and she thrust the gun at him. He took it, then held his arm wide. She walked into his embrace like a ship finding haven after a storm.

"I wasn't going to use it," she said as she buried her head against his chest. A great weight lifted from her heart and floated away. Grief and despair replaced by sorrow tinged with hope.

Lifting her head, she sought the judge's gaze and, upon finding it, reached out to him. He took her hand. The tears he'd kept under control for twenty years welled in his eyes and spilled down his cheeks.

"I tried to erase your past," he said. "I thought the less you knew the better. I tried to keep your grandfather from

ever bringing it up, I tried to make you happy. I was wrong
to ignore it all. I see that now. Can you ever forgive me?"

She brought his hand up to her face and rested her
cheek against his knuckles. "Yes," she whispered.

OUT IN THE BARN, Pete sat down on a straw bale and pulled
Elle onto his lap.

He'd thought he was going to have to save her but, mi-
raculously, she'd saved herself. And in doing that, she'd
saved him. She'd made their future possible. He was so
proud of her he felt like hollering it at the top of his lungs.

He settled for a whisper. "I love you," he said. "Man,
I know I probably shouldn't admit this, but I would have
loved you even if you'd shot Alazandro or pushed him off
a mountain. I just love you. That's all. I can't help it."

Elle laughed softly. "I love you, too," she said, twining
her fingers with his. She added, "I grew up in this barn.
On this ranch. With the judge as my father. But I don't
think I've ever really, truly seen it all, taken it all in,
understood how lucky I was to have it after what had
happened to me—until this moment."

"You were too little. He was clumsy and riddled with
guilt."

"Why did Steve shoot Alazandro?"

"We found Amber's picture in his wallet. He was her
father. She'd been married once, so they had different last
names. The man Steve paid to help him said Steve
believed Alazandro killed his little girl by giving her an
overdose."

"Do you think that's what happened?"

"I don't know," he said. "But Steve was hell-bent on
revenge. He's the one who shot at us the day we left Tahoe."

"I figured. He was late to the airport. What about Rudy?"

"Rudy was apparently an accident. It appears he caught Steve sneaking around Alazandro's place and chased him. According to Steve's helper, Rudy accidentally launched himself into the empty pool. Steve threw a fuse to confuse things."

"Then the man who shot at us that first night and tried to run us off the road?"

"The helper. His job was to take me out while Steve took out Alazandro. Neither one of them was very good at it. They both tried to kidnap you. Steve was in the truck. By the way, the helper saw Alazandro's men dump Jorge in the pool."

"And Shen Kuai?"

"Steve again. He was growing increasingly frustrated because Alazandro never left his apartment where Steve could get a good shot off."

"And Alazandro stayed inside because of the gunshot Steve inflicted."

"Ironic, huh?"

"Revenge is a circle," she whispered.

He kissed her throat. After a pause, he added, "Have you ever been to Santa Barbara?"

"Is that where you're from?"

"Yeah. I think I'd like to get a job on the force there again. I don't want to do undercover work unless it's with you and it's under our covers."

She smiled, then stared him straight in the eye as she said, "I hated lying to you. I'll never do it again."

"Me neither. No more secrets, deal?"

"Deal."

He kissed her face a hundred times in a hundred different places. "I don't suppose there's some little spot out here…some little place where two people in love could spend an uninterrupted night alone?"

"You mean like a hay loft?" she said, drawing back to look at him.

"Yeah," he said, grinning.

"I can think of a spot. Should we tell the judge we'll be gone—"

"No," he said, lifting her in his arms as he stood. She threw her hands around his neck and laughed. "Let's keep it a secret," he added.

"Our secret," she whispered as their lips touched.

"I'M SO GLAD YOU'RE HERE," Scott said the next afternoon.

Elle and Pete stepped into her grandfather's quiet house. Scott's usual good humor looked worn away.

"How is he?"

Scott shook his head. "He asks about you all the time. But he's taking a lot of pain medication, so—"

Elle hugged her grandfather's nurse and then introduced him to Pete. She took Pete's hand and led him into her grandfather's room.

The old man was almost the same color as his bleached sheets. He woke as they approached his bed. His thin lips curved into a smile as Elle sat down on the chair next to the bed and took his frail hand.

"Hi," she said.

He looked from her face to Pete's.

"This is Pete *Walker*, Grandpa," she said, stumbling a little over Pete's real last name. *Jane Ellen Walker. Elle Walker. Not bad.* "He asked me to marry him this morning."

Pete rested his hands on her shoulders as leaned down over her head. "Nice to meet you, sir."

Elle's grandpa said, "What did you tell him, Janey."

She took a second to relive the joy in her heart before saying, "I told him to ask me again in a year."

"You love him?"

"Oh, Grandpa. So much."

His gaze flicked back to Pete as he added, "You'll take good care of my Janey?"

"Yes, sir, I will."

He nodded once, his head barely moving, but Elle saw the pleasure in his pale blue eyes. He tightened his grip on her hand and added, "Víctor Alazandro—"

"Dead," she said.

"Did you—"

"No, Grandpa. I didn't kill him."

"But he did confess?"

Elle looked him straight in the eye. She'd been dithering over this decision since the moment she understood the truth. Did she tell her grandfather his son-in-law killed his daughter and her newborn child?

What was the point to burden the old man as he lay dying?

But didn't he deserve the truth?

She said, "The guilty man has been punished. It's over. They're all at peace now."

He nodded again as his eyes drifted shut.

Elle stayed in her chair, eyes closed, her grandfather's hand clasped in hers. Pete imparted strength just by being there.

She would marry him if he still loved her once he got to know her as a sane woman and not a crazed would-be murderer. They would have children, they would make a family—a family they would both treasure.

Puerta Del Sol. Door of the sun. Isn't that what love was?

She opened her eyes and looked up as Pete leaned down to kiss her.

* * * * *

Enjoy a sneak preview of
MATCHMAKING WITH A MISSION
by B. J. Daniels,
part of the **WHITEHORSE, MONTANA** *miniseries.*
Available from Harlequin Intrigue
in April 2008.

Nate Dempsey has returned to Whitehorse to uncover the truth about his past…

Nate sensed someone watching the house and looked out in surprise to see a woman astride a paint horse just on the other side of the fence. He quickly stepped back from the filthy second-floor window, although he doubted she could have seen him. Only a little of the June sun pierced the dirty glass to glow on the dust-coated floor at his feet as he waited a few heartbeats before he looked out again.

The place was so isolated he hadn't expected to see another soul. Like the front yard, the dirt road was waist-high with weeds. When he'd broken the lock on the back door, he'd had to kick aside a pile of rotten leaves that had blown in from last fall.

As he sneaked a look, he saw that she was still there, staring at the house in a way that unnerved him. He shielded his eyes from the glare of the sun off the dirty window and studied her, taking in her head of long blond hair that feathered out in the breeze from under her Western straw hat.

She wore a tan canvas jacket, jeans and boots. But it

was the way she sat astride the brown-and-white horse that nudged the memory.

He felt a chill as he realized he'd seen her before. In that very spot. She'd been just a kid then. A kid on a pretty paint horse. Not this one—the markings were different. Anyway, it couldn't have been the same horse, considering the last time he had seen her was more than twenty years ago. That horse would be dead by now.

His mind argued it probably wasn't even the same girl. But he knew better. It was the way she sat the horse, so at home in a saddle and secure in her world on the other side of that fence.

To the boy he'd been, she and her horse had represented freedom, a freedom he'd known he would never have—even after he escaped this house.

Nate saw her shift in the saddle, and for a moment he feared she planned to dismount and come toward the house. With Ellis Harper in his grave, there would be little to keep her away.

To his relief, she reined her horse around and rode back the way she'd come.

As he watched her ride away, he thought about the way she'd stared at the house—today and years ago. While the smartest thing she could do was to stay clear of this house, he had a feeling she'd be back.

Finding out her name should prove easy, since he figured she must live close by. As for her interest in Harper House… He would just have to make sure it didn't become a problem.

* * * * *

Be sure to look for
MATCHMAKING WITH A MISSION
and other suspenseful Harlequin Intrigue stories,
available in April wherever books are sold.

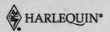

the DEVIL'S footprints

Don't miss the latest thriller from

AMANDA STEVENS

On sale March 2008!

SAVE $1.⁰⁰ off the purchase price of THE DEVIL'S FOOTPRINTS by Amanda Stevens.

Offer valid from March 1, 2008 to May 31, 2008. Redeemable at participating retail outlets. Limit one coupon per purchase.

52608155

5 65373 00076 2   (8100) 0 11460

MAS2530CPN

REQUEST YOUR FREE BOOKS!

2 FREE NOVELS PLUS 2 FREE GIFTS!

 HARLEQUIN®

INTRIGUE®

Breathtaking Romantic Suspense

YES! Please send me 2 FREE Harlequin Intrigue® novels and my 2 FREE gifts (gifts are worth about $10). After receiving them, if I don't wish to receive any more books, I can return the shipping statement marked "cancel." If I don't cancel, I will receive 6 brand-new novels every month and be billed just $4.24 per book in the U.S. or $4.99 per book in Canada, plus 25¢ shipping and handling per book and applicable taxes, if any*. That's a savings of close to 15% off the cover price! I understand that accepting the 2 free books and gifts places me under no obligation to buy anything. I can always return a shipment and cancel at any time. Even if I never buy another book from Harlequin, the two free books and gifts are mine to keep forever.

182 HDN EEZ7 382 HDN EEZK

Name _____ (PLEASE PRINT) _____

Address _____ Apt. # _____

City _____ State/Prov. _____ Zip/Postal Code _____

Signature (if under 18, a parent or guardian must sign)

Mail to the **Harlequin Reader Service:**
IN U.S.A.: P.O. Box 1867, Buffalo, NY 14240-1867
IN CANADA: P.O. Box 609, Fort Erie, Ontario L2A 5X3

Not valid to current subscribers of Harlequin Intrigue books.

Want to try two free books from another line?
Call 1-800-873-8635 or visit www.morefreebooks.com.

* Terms and prices subject to change without notice. N.Y. residents add applicable sales tax. Canadian residents will be charged applicable provincial taxes and GST. This offer is limited to one order per household. All orders subject to approval. Credit or debit balances in a customer's account(s) may be offset by any other outstanding balance owed by or to the customer. Please allow 4 to 6 weeks for delivery. Offer available while quantities last.

Your Privacy: Harlequin is committed to protecting your privacy. Our Privacy Policy is available online at www.eHarlequin.com or upon request from the Reader Service. From time to time we make our lists of customers available to reputable third parties who may have a product or service of interest to you. If you would prefer we not share your name and address, please check here. ☐

Silhouette®
SPECIAL EDITION™

Introducing a brand-new miniseries

Men of
Mercy Medical

Gabe Thorne moved to Las Vegas to open a
new branch of his booming construction
business—and escape from a recent tragedy.
But when his teenage sister showed up pregnant
on his doorstep, he really had his hands full.
Luckily, in turning to Dr. Rebecca Hamilton for
the medical care his sister needed, he found
a cure for himself....

Starting with

THE MILLIONAIRE
AND THE M.D.

by *TERESA SOUTHWICK,*

available in April wherever books are sold.